MELLA AND THE N'ANGA:
AN AFRICAN TALE

D0018470

DATE DUE

BRODART, CO.   Cat. No. 23-221-003

Mella and the N'anga

AN AFRICAN TALE

Gail Nyoka

SUMACH PRESS

To my daughters Lauren and Nadine, with love.

LIBRARY AND ARCHIVES CANADA CATALOGUING IN PUBLICATION

Nyoka, Gail
Mella and the N'anga : an African tale / Gail Nyoka.

ISBN 1-894549-49-X

1. Zimbabwe — Juvenile fiction. I. Title.

PS8627.Y53A66 2005   jC813'.54   C2005-903943-4

ACKNOWLEDGEMENTS

My thanks to Mark Schoenberg, who has helped me through the process,
to Pierre Tetrault, who first saw the potential in the story, and to my editor
Rhea Tregebov for all her help. Also thanks to the Toronto Arts Council
and the Ontario Arts Council for their support.

*Sumach Press acknowledges the support of the Canada Council
for the Arts and the Ontario Arts Council for our publishing program.
We acknowledge the financial support of the Government of Canada through
the Book Publishing Industry Development Program (BPIDP)
for our publishing activities.*

ONTARIO ARTS COUNCIL
CONSEIL DES ARTS DE L'ONTARIO

Printed and bound in Canada

Published by
SUMACH PRESS
1415 Bathurst Street #202
Toronto ON Canada M5R 3H8

sumachpress@on.aibn.com
www.sumachpress.com

PROLOGUE

I am the N'anga. I am called by many names: wise woman, medicine woman, seer, conjurer.

Some say I am as old as the gods, and I will not tell you how many seasons I have walked this earth, nor how I have received my knowledge, which is deep and hot as the molten core of this earth, and high and wide as the stars and the sky.

There are many tales I could tell you; but this one echoes through the ages, and I have chosen to tell it above any other.

For this tale, I must take you back, far in time, to a place we now call Zimbabwe, back to when it did not have that name but was known simply as the Land of the People, when wildebeests thundered across the grasslands in herds so thick they blotted out the landscape. I will take you back to the time of the great hilltop towns, called the madzimbabwe, *that lay within high stone walls, and I will take you back to one such town in particular, the town of Mopopoto.*

I went to this town because I was called. How was I called, you might ask?

If you listen very carefully to the rustle of the grasses, if your ears are attuned to the calling in the leaves — if you know the songs of the breezes, the breezes will tell you when you are being called.

As it blew past my ears, the wind whispered a song that was a cry for help, and the wind told me where that song came from. It was an old, old song, such as had not been heard in a generation or more. It played in my ears and caused me to start my journey.

Long days I travelled. There are those who whisper behind their hands that I take on other forms. The swift-footed cheetah moves with great speed across the grassland, and the graceful eagle soars across hills and rock, eating up miles with her wings across the heights. And so it was that I arrived at the gates of the town just as the sun burst over the hilltop in dazzling brightness.

Chapter 1

THE GIRL WALKED NOISELESSLY, KEEPING TO THE DEEPENING shadows of the stone dividing walls which were still hot to the touch even as evening fell. She knew every curve of the partitioning walls which meandered through these houses at the summit of the hill. The wall provided privacy for those who lived here: the King, his wives and his chief advisors. The Senior Sister, also known as the Great Ancestor, also lived within the King's circle.

A man approached, a member of the King's Guard. The girl stopped, every part of her body tense, hoping that he would not see her. The guard did not peer into the shadows, but walked by without glancing in her direction. When the guard was out of sight, the girl moved on slowly, glad that today she had worn an unadorned indigo-coloured cotton shift with no glitter of gold to betray her presence in the shadows. It was wrapped tightly around her chest and hung in loose folds around her long legs. She was leaner than was thought desirable for the girls of her town, sinuous and taut as a springbok about to leap.

In happier times, this area would be a buzz of activity. There would be petitioners to King Chinembira, praise singers whose songs told of the strengths and virtues of the

King, advisors who would help him run a kingdom that encompassed much land and many smaller chiefdoms throughout the countryside. But these were not happy times. Members of the King's Guard still watched and marched, but inside the great house, King Chinembira lay unmoving on his bed, his skin ashen, his once-powerful frame shrunken and wasted.

The girl ached to see the King, but today that had been forbidden by the Vahozi, King Chinembira's senior wife. The Vahozi had called yet another n'anga to cure the King. This one was said to have delivered spectacular cures and had come a long distance. The girl had seen the man enter the King's house hours ago. He had entered, but had not come out. The girl stared at the chevron-decorated walls of the house that faced her across the hardened, grassless earth of the compound. The house stared silently back, denying her the knowledge she craved of what was going on inside. Would this doctor be the one to save the King?

There had been too many disappointments: n'angas who had come, pondered, tried their medicines and remedies, only to pronounce the King incurable. The King was going to die, a drawn-out death that stretched from weeks to months. But that was not the worst of it. For every day and every week that went by, the land, tied to the guardianship and health of the King, sickened as he did. Both King and land were wasting away, little by little.

The tear that rolled down the girl's cheek and splashed to the ground was swallowed instantly by the dry dust. She quickly wiped away others that threatened to fall. Tonight there was a visit to be made, a visit to someone other than the King. There was a tremble in the girl's step as, still keeping to the shadows, she made her way towards the next house, that of Rangarirai, the Senior Sister.

The Senior Sister wasn't really the King's sister. Senior Sister was the name given to the oldest woman in the King's clan, and Rangarirai was very old indeed. In fact, she was the oldest person in the entire kingdom. Her opinion was sought by the King and she was much revered.

The most difficult part of remaining unseen was in crossing the open ground to the Senior Sister's house. The girl did not want to draw attention to herself by running, but she quickened her pace as she stepped away from the shadows. Even in the gathering darkness, the girl could see the herringbone designs painted on the outside of Rangarirai's house, the pale tan colouring contrasting with the deep dark brown of the hard-mud walls.

Rangarirai lived alone. Her husband had died very young. She had had only one daughter, and she, too, had died a long time ago in the collapse of one of the gold mines. Many women had died in that disaster, because it was the women of the tribe who descended into the earth to work the mines.

At Rangarirai's door, the girl stopped, calling softly, "Senior Sister, I have come."

"Come in, King's Daughter."

Mella, she who was the king's daughter, pushed aside the water buffalo skin that covered the opening to the doorway.

"You were not seen?" Rangarirai asked.

"No, Great Ancestor."

"That is good. It is well that there are no questions. This visit must remain a secret between us."

Mella breathed in the scent of the sweet herbs that hung in bunches from the roof of Rangarirai's house. Her eyes roamed the decorated clay pots that lined the shelves molded into the walls of the house. What could the Senior Sister have in mind? The unspoken question was expressed in her wide, soft brown eyes. There was a hint of defiance in her face that was accentuated by Mella's arched eyebrows and high forehead. She had clear, smooth skin. Her face was softened by bow-shaped lips and a halo of curly hair cut in a neat round. On some occasions, her hair would be woven into intricate braids, but today, it fanned around her head like rays from the sun.

"Sit down, King's Daughter," Rangarirai said with a nod of her head.

Mella took a place on the reed mat on the floor of the house, while the Senior Sister lowered herself onto a carved wooden stool with the aid of her walking stick. Mella had always admired this stick for the carved snake that curled its way up the smooth wooden shaft, the lifelike head stopping just short of the rounded handle at the top. Mella looked up into the lined and weathered face of the Senior Sister.

"Your father's illness is very mysterious," continued Rangarirai. "We know that the ruler is always the guardian of the land. The ancestors tell us that the condition of the land is a reflection of his guardianship. We see the land dying.

We see our food and water rationed. We see the approach of starvation, suffering and death."

Mella nodded reluctantly. Had her father done something to cause this failure of the rains? She felt compelled to defend him. "But he has always been a just ruler."

"Even so," said Rangarirai, "there are certain traditions that have been lost in our kingdom, not just in your father's time, but by the ruler before him. This is not the time to speak of all the things that have been lost. We will talk of these another time. But now you, Mella, may have the chance to save both your father and our people."

"Surely you are only teasing me, Senior Sister," stammered Mella. Did the Senior Sister tell her to come here in secret just to make fun of her? "If I knew how to save my father, I would have done so many weeks ago."

"You do not yet know how to save him, but you will learn. You must show a willingness to be brave. There is one who can tell us the cause of your father's illness, and who will be able to cure him. She is the Great N'anga of whom you have heard in the stories."

"I have heard those stories," agreed Mella, "but everyone knows that they are just stories told to children. If the Great N'anga truly existed, the Vahozi and the Chief Councillor would have sent for her."

"The people have forgotten. They chose not to listen and now they have forgotten." Rangarirai's tone surprised Mella by its vehemence. She would have questioned Rangarirai, but remembered how the Vahozi, the King's senior wife, had chided Mella for her questions. Since Mella's mother died, her Aunt Tongai had held the title of Vahozi.

"Mella of the Runaway Mouth," the Vahozi had called her, and "Mella of the Runaway Legs." Neither trait was considered suitable for a girl, especially for one who must make a match with a future ruler of one of the neighbouring clans. Mella's questions did not please the Vahozi.

"This N'anga can only be reached if one knows how to call her," continued the Senior Sister. She paused to make sure that Mella was listening. "I am the only person in the kingdom left who knows how to call the N'anga. I am the only one who knows the song."

Mella could keep her questions to herself no longer. "Then why have you not called the N'anga?"

"I am the last one," Rangarirai said by way of explanation, although Mella found it an unsatisfactory one.

Rangarirai paused, as if in reflection. A faraway look came to her eyes. "There must always be more than one who can sing the song." She resumed her speech suddenly with an urgency. "The song must have a force greater than one person's voice and soul. But amongst the people there is great fear of the song and what it can bring." She leaned down closer to Mella. "I can teach you the song, King's Daughter, although it is forbidden."

"You would teach me something that is forbidden?"

"I will teach you, if you wish to save your father."

Mella searched the lines and crevices that marked the face of Rangarirai. The Senior Sister wished to teach her a song that was forbidden. She would learn. She saw in Rangarirai's face the expression of a long life lived with both pain and joy. Mella knew that the Senior Sister was a person she could trust. It did not take her long to answer. "Yes. Yes," she said again. "I will sing the song if you will teach me."

A slow smile played around the edges of Rangarirai's mouth. "I see that I was right to believe that you would be the one. We must call the N'anga tonight, but we will go separately to the forest. Meet me at the track that leads to the Tumbling Waters."

Mella knew the place well, although tumbling waters no longer raced over the rocky ledge. The waters had slowed almost to nothing, while elsewhere in the land other water sources had dried up altogether.

The Senior Sister stood and made her way to her doorway. "I will go directly," she told Mella. "And you will circle around. Wait here for a while and let no-one see you leave my house."

Mella listened to the soft tap of the Senior Sister's stick on the hard ground, and then waited in the stillness of Rangarirai's house. No-one would ever question where the Great Ancestor chose to go, for she was the living representative of those who watched over the welfare of the people.

Mella hoped the ancestors would be pleased by her decision to listen to the Senior Sister. She waited in the silence of Rangarirai's house. Time seemed to move very slowly, but Mella knew that she would get to the meeting place at much greater speed than Rangarirai, and she wanted to leave enough time that their leaving the walled town would not arouse suspicion. Mella frequently went alone into the forest, although it displeased her Aunt Tongai, the Vahozi.

When she could wait no longer, Mella stood and carefully pushed aside the door covering. She peered outside. The moon was now up, casting a silver light, but no-one was in sight. The King's illness combined with the water and food shortages seemed to have made the spirit of the people shrink, so that they kept more to the security of their houses. They did not gather to talk and laugh as they had done before. Mella left Rangarirai's house as she had come, keeping quietly to the shadows. Once she reached the streets where the townsfolk lived, she walked freely, as if on one of her usual visits to the forest.

Had anyone been near the place called the Tumbling Waters later that night, they might have seen two figures with their faces turned upwards towards the moon that hung high over the falls. They might have seen these figures stretch out their arms as if to touch the rays of light sent down by the moon, the symbol of the goddess Bomu Rambi. They would have heard the forbidden song sung in the name of the goddess. They would have heard the thin cracked voice of Rangarirai and they would have heard a hesitant younger voice repeating the phrases many times. Over and over again they would have heard the pitch and tone corrected. Then they would have heard two voices joined, the old and the young. The young voice they would have heard grow stronger in a song that caused even the baboons to stir and clamber high into tree branches as the melody wafted over the very tops of those trees like the fluttering of new leaves.

Chapter 2

MELLA WAS STARTING TO HAVE HER DOUBTS ABOUT THE existence of the N'anga. Perhaps she was only a legend after all. Or perhaps the Senior Sister had not remembered the song correctly. How long would it take the N'anga to come, if she came at all?

Mella climbed the stone steps which hugged the high walls that surrounded the town of Mopopoto. The walls stood solid and commanding, over ten metres high, and thick enough that guards could walk their length between four towers spaced to face the four directions.

This was the second afternoon Mella had climbed these steps and looked out over the expanse of brown, sun-baked land that stretched beyond. Even sheltered by the shade of the large overlapping leaves that formed the parapet roof, Mella was hot. The afternoon sun beat through the open sides, forcing Mella to stay close to the centre post where she was in the deepest shade. Once Mella ventured to the waist-high stone wall surrounding the parapet, leaning over the side for a better look into the distance. She pulled away instantly, rubbing her hand where she had touched the searing hot stones. Even the huge soapstone birds perched at intervals along the top of the walls seemed almost to droop as waves of heat shimmered off their hard, immobile bodies. The birds represented the watchful spirits of the ancestors. Were the ancestors' spirits still guarding the people?

In the distance, vultures hung in the sky. Mella, seeing no sign of anybody approaching, started back down the stairs. She didn't want to make it obvious that she was waiting for someone to arrive. She would not look again.

The steps were steep but, pushing away her disappointment, Mella started to run down. Wherever she went Mella ran, especially if she had the chance to go into the forest. She stopped abruptly when she saw her Aunt Tongai, the Vahozi, arms folded, waiting at the bottom of the steps. The Vahozi was a large, formidable woman, the tallest woman in the town.

"Mella," boomed the Vahozi in her sonorous voice. "What are you doing up there?"

"I was looking at the land, my aunt. It's all so dry."

"Looking at it won't make the rains come. You are to do the sewing that I asked of you, you lazy girl."

"Yes, Aunt Tongai." For the thousandth time, Mella wished that her mother was still alive. It was Mella's mother who had once borne the title of Vahozi. Mella had accepted that the title now belonged to her mother's younger sister, Tongai. She only wished that her aunt shared some of her mother's kind nature. Mella remembered that her mother had gentle hands and a beautiful singing voice. She remembered when her mother and father and brother had all sung together. Everything had changed after her mother's death, and now there was no more singing as a family. Those times together seemed like such a long time ago. These days Mella hardly even spoke to Dikita, her brother, who kept himself aloof from her. Mella followed her aunt back up the hill to the Vahozi's house. As chief wife, Tongai had a large house next to the King's. The Vahozi had fine cloth that she wanted made into dresses. The cloth had been bought from traders before the hard times had befallen the kingdom, and the Vahozi now had assigned Mella the task of sewing the cloth into dresses. She would personally supervise Mella's work to make sure that the stitching was fine and straight and small. The Vahozi had exacting standards for everything: she took her position as Senior Wife seriously.

Sometimes Aunt Tongai had Mella sweep the house, fetch water from the well or take the laundry to the river. Even though Mella was the King's daughter, Aunt Tongai wanted to make sure that Mella was able to do all these tasks as well as any other girl. It was proper for every young woman to know her domestic duties.

Mella worked at her sewing until it was time to help with preparations for the evening meal. Chunks of meat were mixed into cornmeal to make the stew that was their customary supper. Like all meals, portions were smaller now than in the times of plenty that Mella had known before. The adults ate first and then, finally, Mella had her chance to eat. However, she was still not free to go to visit her father until all the bowls had been cleaned and put away.

After her chores were done, Mella ran to her father's house where she greeted her older cousin who, as the King's niece, had the duty of caring for the King in his illness. This was a job that was traditionally shared by the King's nieces. Mella hesitated before she entered the room where her father lay. What would she see this time? He looked more like a skeleton every time she came. As she entered, she saw that his lips were cracked and bleeding. Mella dabbed a damp cloth to his mouth.

"If the N'anga comes, you will speak wise judgements again," whispered Mella, thinking of the many petitioners who used to come with their disputes. They still came, but were now seen by Ganyambadzi, King Chinembira's chief Councillor. The King's Chief Councillor was a very important man who often settled affairs for the King. Now that the King was unable to move or even to speak, Ganyambadzi made all the decisions in his place.

The King's eyes fluttered open at the sound of Mella's voice, but the lids closed over them again before Mella had finished speaking. Had her father understood her words? Mella touched his hand, which felt as fragile as a dry leaf. "Does the Great N'anga really exist, Father?"

The King remained silent.

Mella left the room, nodding once more to her cousin. She made her way to the sleeping hut, which was shared by all the girls in Mella's age grouping. The girls born within a time which covered a period of four rainy seasons moved into the sleeping hut when they were old enough. Each year the oldest group left the hut for homes of their own and were replaced by a younger set of girls.

The boys who were approaching maturity had their own shared sleeping house that stood on the far side of the compound. Mella never went there, but she often thought of Dikita. Her older brother had recently been made a member of the King's Guard and had moved from the boys' house to the house for the unmarried members of the King's Guard.

Mella fell asleep thinking of the proud look of the new guards as they stood for the first time in the leopard-skin tunic cut to hang over one shoulder and clasped with a pin. Each bent forward to receive the tall plume that was placed on his head by the King as a symbol of his new status.

@

This morning there was something different in the air. Mella sensed it as soon as she woke up. It was still very early, yet there was a buzz that was unusual. Some of the other girls had also woken, alert to the activity outside their sleeping quarters. Mella caught the eye of Shamiso. Shamiso was a little younger than Mella, a girl with a pretty oval face and eyes that were a velvet brown. She was short and compact and wore her hair in braids that were tipped by small cowry shells. Shamiso was shy and often solitary. She glanced at Mella, a look of concern on her face. Mella knew at once that Shamiso had the same fear as herself. Could the King have died?

Mella dressed quickly and hurried outside, ahead of the other young women who were also getting into their day clothes. People hurried towards the King's house in a general state of agitation and apprehension. No-one spoke to Mella as she rushed to her father's house. A crowd gathered outside and attention was focused on the surprising figure who stood calmly outside the door. She was a woman unlike any other. Mella edged forward to get a closer look although, like everybody else, she kept a respectful distance, leaving a wide circle of space around the stranger.

This woman was taller even than the Vahozi. She was unstooped, and the black ostrich plumes she wore on her head made her look taller still. The N'anga — for it was she — gave the impression of great age and great calm. Her face bore no lines. Mella knew her own skin was of the darkest brown. But the N'anga's skin was so black it looked like midnight. Her hair was cut short and was also very black. Cupped in her palm, the N'anga held four short pieces of bone. Still keeping her back very straight, the N'anga squatted to the ground. Mella watched as the N'anga's long fingers opened and the bones arced through the air, falling to the ground in a pattern which the N'anga studied carefully. All eyes were on the N'anga as she picked up the bones and threw them again. What could the patterns made by the bones mean? The N'anga repeated the action twice, three times, then once again before she carefully put the bones back into the pouch at her side and stood to address the townspeople.

Now Mella saw that Ganyambadzi, the King's Chief Councillor, had been standing by all this time, not far from the N'anga. He moved forward to address the N'anga.

"Wise One, what have the bones told you?" he asked.

The N'anga replied to Ganyambadzi in a voice that was clear enough for all to hear. "I have seen the cause of King

Chinembira's illness, and I have seen the sacrifice that must be made for his cure."

Sacrifice. The word lodged ominously in Mella's mind. A sacrifice would have to be made.

There was no sound from the gathered people, not even a cry from one of the young children or babies.

"We await your instructions, Wise One," said Ganyambadzi.

Mella saw the N'anga look from Ganyambadzi to the other faces around her, then from the Vahozi and the Senior Sister to the warriors who stood in ordered rows to either side of the King's compound, and to the assorted people in the crowd. Surely the N'anga had not picked out Mella? Yet it appeared that the N'anga was looking straight at her. Mella felt uncomfortable under the gaze of the N'anga. People in the crowd shuffled and waited for the N'anga to speak.

Finally, the N'anga was ready. "The message comes from Bomu Rambi herself."

There was a collective gasp. This must indeed be an exceptional n'anga if it were true that the goddess of the people spoke through her. But no-one doubted that this n'anga could receive the message of the goddess.

"Bomu Rambi has sent the King's illness as a sign of her displeasure," continued the N'anga. "The illness and the blight upon the land cannot easily be taken away because you have neglected the practices that maintain the harmony of the lands. There is only one way the King can be cured, and that is through the powers of the Python Healer. One of you must go to the cave of the Python Healer and bring the creature here to heal the King."

It was as if time stood still. No-one moved, no-one spoke. No man or woman dared to look into the eyes of the N'anga or into the face of a neighbour.

The N'anga's voice broke the spell of silence and stillness that was over all. "Is there anyone who will go to the cave of the Python?" she asked. "If no-one will undertake this journey, the King will die and the kingdom will fall."

"I will go." Mella pushed forward until she was at the front of the crowd, facing the N'anga. "I will bring the Python to cure my father."

At once there was a well of sound as all the people found their voices again.

Ganyambadzi held up his hand for quiet and addressed Mella. "Are you aware, King's Daughter, that no person within living memory has been to the cave of the Python Healer and returned?"

Mella nodded even though she felt a weakness that threatened to make her knees buckle as she stood. Stories were told of the Python, who lived in a cave of treasures. It had been many years since anyone had gone in search of the Python's treasures because those who went never came back.

The N'anga showed no sign of emotion at Mella's offer to go to the Python. "You must leave today," she said.

"Wait." A shout came from the ranks of the warriors. Mella's brother, Dikita, stepped forward, followed closely by his friend, Chiboro.

"Excuse us, Wise One," said Dikita, with a slight bow of

acknowledgement to the N'anga. "It is the job of warriors to accomplish this task. I will go with Chiboro."

"Indeed, Wise One," agreed Chiboro. "Such an important task cannot be left to a girl."

The N'anga gave them a glance that was so cold they both took a step backward. Yet even as they did so, excitement moved through the crowd. Voices were raised in relief that the King's son would undertake the task.

Today the warriors were without their ceremonial plumes, but Dikita and Chiboro made an impressive sight. Their leopard-skin tunics fitted over muscular bodies. Dikita was the taller and stronger of the two, while Chiboro gave the impression of agility and determination. Chiboro had a full mouth in a lively face. He had been named the Great Talker. But Mella had never liked him. All that talk — Mella believed that Chiboro's talk had turned her brother away from her.

Chiboro was speaking again, his words tumbling over each other in his haste. "We warriors have the speed and strength to reach the Python's cave and bring the Python Healer back here to save the King. It is only because we were considering the enormity of this job that we paused so that it was Mella who stepped forward first with her childish offer. But, of course, Chief Councillor, it would be foolishness for her to go."

Mella felt the sting of humiliation rising through her cheeks. She turned to Ganyambadzi. "Chief Councillor, our journey would be the better if we all went to the cave of the Python," she said.

"No. It is not possible to take you. You would slow us down and get in our way," interrupted Chiboro.

"We need to go without Mella," said Dikita.

Ganyambadzi turned to Mella. "It is the right and duty of the warriors to go and to accomplish their task in the way that they need and wish to do. Dikita and Chiboro will leave today."

"This is a job for warriors," Chiboro hissed at Mella. She could hear the contempt in his voice and see his look of complete disdain.

Hot shame burned within Mella. Keeping her head high, and with as much dignity as she could manage, she excused herself and walked back through the crowd. She didn't dare glance at the N'anga. She kept on walking until she reached the town walls, her thoughts focused on the way Chiboro had, once again, made her feel foolish and small. This time not just in front of her brother but in front of the entire town. She would have liked to leave the confines of the walls and run to the privacy and comfort of the forest. But she would have to wait to see Dikita and Chiboro start their journey before she could get away. How long would it take them to prepare for such a journey?

Mella looked up to the sky, already hazy with heat over the tops of the walls. She would climb the stone stairway once more, where she would be away from the townspeople. The guards would nod their courteous greeting and then they would turn away. It would be as if there was nobody there in all the world, except herself. With her long legs, she easily bounded up the steep steps, anxious to reach the top.

From this vantage point, the excited talk of the assembled townspeople was diminished to a low hum. She looked down on their figures as they gathered in groups to talk about the N'anga's extraordinary address to them. Some people had gathered in the large central meeting place, the *dare,* under the shade of the ancient msasa tree that spread its branches across the assembly point. Others were walking along the stone pathways that wound through the town between the smaller stone walls that separated the homes and courtyards of the important people. Mella looked down on the grass-thatched conical rooftops of the houses. Her father's house was clearly visible, separate from the others, situated on the highest point of the hill. Beside it stood a stone tower, carved to look like the skin of a crocodile. The crocodile was important because it helped to cause rain and lived in contact with the ancestor spirit world at the bottom of sacred pools. The tower, shaped like a grain bin, reminded the people that the King was responsible for the fertility of the land. The goddess Bomu Rambi brought good harvests to the land as long as the king ruled well. But now the King lay ill, the soil no longer brought food and even the cows failed to produce milk.

There was a part of Mella that was glad she didn't have to make such a dangerous journey. The stories about the Python Healer warned that the Python demanded a sacrifice for any act of healing. Perhaps she would never have made it back to the town with the Python. Perhaps the Python would have killed her right away. Certainly her brother Dikita had not thought her capable of such a task. Perhaps he was right. They all knew she could not bring back the Python Healer.

With these thoughts, Mella waited until, at last, she saw the two young warriors ready to start their journey. There they were, striding through the gate, looking neither back nor to the sides, seemingly oblivious to the encouragement shouted to them by the townsfolk gathered at the gate to see them off.

Mella was still angry at them. She would live forever with the humiliation that they had brought to her. Yet they may have saved her from death. She thought they looked the perfect warriors, proud, bold and determined. Slung across their bodies on leather straps, their water gourds and bark-cloth bags contained enough food for their journey. In their hands they held their iron-bladed spears. They seemed invincible. If they were successful, her father would be healed and rain would come to the parched land. Clouds and cooling breezes would bring an end to the relentless burning of the sun. And her father's life would be saved.

Mella continued to watch as Dikita and Chiboro made their way along the twisting pathway that wound past the modest round houses that belonged to some of the ordinary people who lived outside the town walls. The warriors walked on past the cultivated fields where the women grew crops of maize and plantain, past the pits and enclosures for the cattle and further, on and on. With lithe, easy steps they quickly covered the ground that led to the plains that spread before them in the distance, brown and dry, stretching to the horizon and beyond.

As Mella watched, one of the distant figures turned to look back. Mella thought it must be Dikita. Would he know that she was watching him? Ever since he had joined the King's Guard, Dikita had taken little notice of Mella. She doubted he would look for her. The young boy who had once joined in her games had fled into the tough shell of the warrior who sought accolades and basked in the flattery of ambitious companions, especially Chiboro.

"Mella, Daughter of the King."

Mella was startled out of her thoughts. She looked down to see the N'anga calling her.

"We must speak. Come down."

Mella didn't dare disobey, though she didn't want to leave the watch tower and go back to the scene of her humiliation. Still, she would have to leave sooner or later. When the N'anga called, it was wise to do as she was asked. The N'anga had a great many powers.

Mella ran down the curving stone steps, lightly touching the sides of the walls to steady herself. Her heart was beating fast when she came to a stop at the bottom of the steps — not from the exertion of the run but because she would have to face the N'anga. She had to look up at the N'anga, whose cold, still eyes were staring down at her. Not only did the N'anga have the darkest eyes of anyone Mella had ever seen, those eyes possessed an inner flame that sometimes flickered and sometimes dimmed. Either way, to look into the eyes of the N'anga was to look into a space without end. Mella had to stop herself from trembling as she stood in front of her.

"King's Daughter, it was your voice that called me," said the N'anga.

Mella wasn't sure if this were an accusation. The N'anga's tone was neutral.

"Yes, Wise One," Mella answered. "I hoped that you would cure my father."

"Where did you learn that song? No-one knows how to sing it any more."

"The Senior Sister still remembers," said Mella. "She is the only person in all the land who knows the song, and she taught it to me".

"Ah, yes," said the N'anga. "It is lucky for you that your Great Ancestor remembered. It seems that your people have too long ignored the Senior Sister's warnings."

Mella felt uncomfortable under the unwavering stare of the N'anga. It was as if the N'anga was looking into her mind and wanted to discern her every thought. Maybe the N'anga could do just that.

"I have heard," said Mella, "that before she became the Senior Sister, Rangarirai was almost sent from the town because she spoke of things that she should not."

"And what things were those?"

"I don't know. It was before I was born. But I have heard Aunt Tongai speak of it with some of the other women. I was not supposed to hear."

"You did well to listen to the Senior Sister and to learn the forbidden song."

"But now it is Dikita who will be called a hero." Mella knew that she could never tell anyone of her part in bringing the N'anga who had found the cure for her father.

"He will be a hero only if he returns with the Python Healer," the N'anga answered, softly.

It had not occurred to Mella that Dikita and Chiboro could possibly fail to bring the Python Healer. But what price would they have to pay for the Python's help? "Well, of course, they must bring the Python Healer," she said. "My father must not be allowed to die, and I do not want Dikita or Chiboro to die either. Do you believe the Python Healer would kill them?"

"Whether they are harmed or whether they are not depends upon they themselves."

"But what do you mean?" asked Mella.

"They must approach her with true courage."

"They are strong and brave," said Mella. "I think they were right not to want to take me. I'm afraid of the Python."

"True courage comes from the heart," said the N'anga. "You have much to learn." She looked at Mella even more intently than before. "Much to learn. And I will be your teacher."

"Oh!" Mella was too surprised to say anything more. It seemed to Mella that the N'anga almost smiled at Mella's reaction. In her confusion, Mella felt a flush of excitement and a tinge of fear.

"How could I learn from you?" Mella stammered. "I am not a magician or a healer. I am the King's daughter, and soon my aunt will find a prince whom I must marry." Mella bit her lip. She had spoken when she shouldn't, as usual. Her aunt would have called her Mella of the Runaway Mouth again if she had heard her. It was good that her aunt was not within sight. Aunt Tongai was very strict about how girls were to behave. Mella was to keep silent except when spoken to and to stay within the confines of the enclosure. Mella chafed at her aunt's rules. She would escape whenever she could to the forest, where she loved to walk and listen to the birds and monkeys, or climb the trees. Mella made sure no-one saw her climbing trees, so they wouldn't tell her aunt.

Mella was afraid the N'anga would be offended by what she had said, but the N'anga showed neither offence nor approval.

"Marriage? Is that what you want of your life?" The N'anga asked.

"No!" Mella answered without hesitation. "I do not want to marry yet. When my mother was alive, she said I did not have to. But Aunt Tongai says that I must, to help unite the kingdom. She is my father's senior wife now and I must do as she says."

"Does the welfare of the kingdom not interest you?" asked the N'anga.

"Certainly it does," said Mella. "Does that mean I must marry?"

"Not at all," answered the N'anga. "There are much more important things that you must learn and put into practice, if you are worthy and you are willing. Indeed, they are vital to the kingdom."

"Yes, yes, I'm willing, and I'll try to be worthy." Anything would be better than being married to someone now. If

Mella were not so afraid of the N'anga, she would have clapped for joy. What would the N'anga teach her?

"First," said the N'anga. "We must find the Senior Sister and your father's Chief Councillor. They must help."

The N'anga sent one of the children to find Ganyambadzi, and together Mella and the N'anga walked to Rangarirai's house.

Mella liked to walk through the town by the side of the N'anga. All who saw them stood back in awe, and Mella was pleased to see that not one single person approached to tell her she'd been wrong in her wish to undertake the journey to the Python Healer with Dikita and Chiboro.

Even though she was bursting with questions, Mella thought it best not to pester the N'anga. She couldn't imagine talking to the N'anga in the ordinary way. Aunt Tongai would be surprised to see her so quiet now. Mella couldn't suppress the smile that came to her face and made her eyes sparkle under their long lashes. She was starting to feel better already.

Mella looked searchingly at her father's house as they walked by. She still couldn't get used to the unnatural quiet surrounding this area, even after weeks of King Chinembira's illness.

Soon the quiet would be broken. When Dikita and Chiboro returned with the Python Healer, her father would sit on his specially carved wooden stool in his fine robes, and all around him there would be well-wishers, music, singing and feasting. Mella longed for the return of such a time when the trees would bear fruit, and when meat and milk would be plentiful.

The N'anga did not slacken her pace. She carried on, past the partition that separated the dwellings of the King from the rest of the town, to the side with herringbone patterns at the boundary of the Senior Sister's area.

Inside, Rangarirai's house offered a cool respite from the heat. Rangarirai leaned on her snake-carved walking stick, her face a smile of welcome. She gave Mella the kind of look that said, *You see, I was right.*

Mella returned the Senior Sister's smile. In the comfort of Rangarirai's trust in her, Mella could forget about her earlier embarrassment and be glad that she had trusted the Great Ancestor.

"Greetings, Wise One," Ganyambadzi called when he arrived at the doorway. If he was surprised to see Mella with Rangarirai and the N'anga, he did not show it. He greeted Rangarirai and Mella in turn.

The N'anga wasted no time in getting to her point. "I have brought you here on a grave matter," she stated.

Rangarirai nodded. Ganyambadzi, however, glanced over at Mella as if questioning why she would be there. Still, he said nothing and waited for the N'anga to continue. Mella held her breath. What would the N'anga say?

"I have told you what must be done to save the King," said the N'anga. "But that is not the whole story. No, not by half."

Mella could see the look of alarm that crossed Ganyambadzi's face. The N'anga did not say anything further. She seemed disinclined to elaborate. At last, Ganyambadzi broke the silence.

"You have told us, Wise One, that only the Python Healer could save the King. And you have said that the kingdom would fall if the King were not healed."

The N'anga nodded, but seemed to be waiting for something more.

Mella looked from face to face, wondering what would happen next. Rangarirai surely knew what the N'anga meant. It was indeed Rangarirai who spoke next.

"The Wise One has also told us that the cause of the King's illness, the drought and all the misfortunes that have come upon us is that we have disregarded the ways of Bomu Rambi."

Mella had almost forgotten what Rangarirai had told her.

"That is correct," said the N'anga, nodding again. "This is the root of the problem, and this is what we must remedy. There is much to be done in a short time, and for this we must depend on Mella."

Chapter 3

"WHAT WERE YOU DOING ALL DAY WITH THE OLD PEOPLE?" Revai asked. Revai was one of the girls who shared the sleeping hut with Mella. Mella liked Revai; she was open and intelligent. Mella also knew that she could trust Revai not to flatter her just because she was the King's daughter. Sometimes Mella wondered if she had any real friends, or if the other girls thought only of her position. Revai was not as tall as Mella, but she was a commanding figure. She was muscular and strong with striking features — a wide mouth that often mocked, eyes wide and large, but which held a seriousness under their thick brows. Revai wore her hair clipped close to her perfectly shaped head. Most people didn't know what to make of Revai and her searching questions. She was quick to dismiss anyone or anything she thought false or foolish.

There was giggling from the other girls in the sleeping hut where the group was settling in for the night. Revai often shocked and delighted the other girls with her daring irreverence. She only did this in the safety of the girls' sleeping hut, where secrets were shared and stories told with no danger of anyone else hearing them.

"Shh, Revai," said Shamiso. "The ancestors will punish you."

"Maybe the N'anga will contact them and ask them to take Revai," said another girl. "Weren't you scared being with the N'anga, Mella?"

"A little," said Mella. "But the N'anga has so much to teach me. She told me that the reason I was not to go to the cave of the Python is because I must be here to learn about the Daughters of the Hunt."

"Daughters of the Hunt?" said Revai. "Who are they?"

"The Senior Sister says that they were part of our tribe long ago," said Mella. "The N'anga says it is a tradition we must bring back. If we do not, the kingdom will die, even if Dikita and Chiboro find the Python."

The sounds of shuffling and fidgeting came to a stop. In the almost-darkness of the sleeping hut, all eyes turned to Mella.

Mella sat up and drew her knees up to her chest. There had been so much talk about the N'anga, Dikita and Chiboro, that Mella was pleased to have this chance to tell the others about what she had learned that afternoon.

"The N'anga said that our tribe once had a group of young women called the Daughters of the Hunt. They were very special to Bomu Rambi. Rangarirai remembers them from when she was very young. But the Daughters were disbanded. The people thought that they were uncontrollable and that they were a bad example for the girls of the tribe. After that, it was forbidden for girls to play the special drum and to learn the arts of the hunt."

"Girls played the drum?" Shamiso's voice was eager. "I would love to play the drum."

"It would be wonderful," said Revai. "Think of how we would shake the town with our sounds."

"But we have never been allowed even to approach the drums. Could we really play? Does this drum still exist?" asked Shamiso.

"Rangarirai still has the drum," said Mella. "It was given to her for safekeeping. She has kept it hidden all these years."

Revai let out a whoop of joy.

"Quiet, Revai," cautioned the other girls.

"Can we see the drum? What is it like?" asked one.

"We cannot see it yet," said Mella, "but soon we will have the chance. Some of us will learn to play. The N'anga said we must bring back the Daughters of the Hunt or Bomu Rambi will abandon our people and the kingdom will fall."

"Then we must bring back the Daughters," said Shamiso. "But how?"

"The N'anga will start to teach me," said Mella. "And Ganyambadzi has agreed to teach the art of the bow to three of us. We will learn the secrets of the forest and the animals. Two more and myself will be chosen as the first and, later, there will be more."

"Who are the other two?" Revai asked.

"I don't know," answered Mella. "Tomorrow, the N'anga will decide."

"I hope it's me," said one girl.

"Ha! Why would the N'anga choose you?" said another. "I wonder what she will teach us."

"I wouldn't want to be taught by the N'anga."

"No. You never know what she would do."

"What about learning to be a huntress?"

"That would be wonderful."

"What if you were in the forest and a leopard jumped down on you from the trees?"

Opinions and thoughts were whispered throughout the sleeping hut for some time before the girls fell asleep. Some of the girls sounded apprehensive, but Mella felt a tingle of excitement as she anticipated the day to come.

@

Mella's eyes flickered open. She knew it was early. Light was only just starting to filter through the crack in the doorway. Quietly, so as not to disturb any of the others, she got up and slipped out the door. She was too excited to sleep, and she liked these early mornings when no-one else was about. Rangarirai's stories of the Daughters of the Hunt, who went freely to the bush and spent nights under the stars, were so wonderful. The Daughters wore the symbol of the crescent moon. *They* didn't spend *their* time cooking or cleaning or doing anybody else's sewing!

"Are you going to the forest today?"

Mella turned around in surprise to see Shamiso standing behind her.

"I have seen you go to the forest in the mornings," Shamiso said with a tentative smile.

"I did not know you were awake," said Mella.

"I am often awake early," said Shamiso. "And I see you

when you go to the forest. I would have liked to go too, but you always run so fast. Perhaps you don't want anyone to come with you."

Mella shrugged. "You may come if you wish to. Just as long as you do not tell Aunt Tongai what I do."

"I promise I won't." Shamiso breathed in the morning air and looked around her. "I love the morning. I love its sounds of waking birds, and its smells, like fresh beginnings. I want to go to the forest with you for those green-of-morning smells and the colours-of-morning flowers."

"I love the same things as you," said Mella quietly, looking at Shamiso as if she were seeing her for the first time. Mella had had no idea that Shamiso's thoughts echoed her own. "Do you also like to climb trees?"

Shamiso gave a soft laugh, quiet, yet full of joy. Her white, even teeth showed in a smile that she did not often share. Her smile made her dark eyes shine and her cheeks dimple. "I would like to try," said Shamiso. "I am glad that you have given me permission to come with you."

"I will be glad to have your company." Mella smiled back. Here was a friend who liked her for herself and not just because she was the daughter of the King. Mella knew that Shamiso was loyal and giving to those few whom she chose to befriend.

"We will go to the forest together," said Mella. "But we cannot go there this morning. I think that the N'anga will call us even before the morning meal."

Mella sat down at the base of a marula tree, although its leaves were now so withered it offered no shade at all, and there was no sign of its bright red berries. Shamiso sat down beside her, raking her fingers through the dusty ground.

"I can tell how much you want to be a Daughter of the Hunt," said Shamiso.

Mella turned to look at Shamiso. Should she tell her what she had been thinking? She felt she could trust Shamiso to keep her secret thoughts.

"When I am one of the Daughters," said Mella, "my father will notice me and see that I am as good as Dikita."

"The King spent many hours with Dikita before he became ill."

"He wanted Dikita to be a good warrior. Now I will be able to throw a spear myself."

"That will be good," said Shamiso. "But I think there must be more to being a Daughter of the Hunt than throwing a spear or knowing how to fight and kill. I think that the real reason for the Daughters is to learn the mysteries of Bomu Rambi."

"It's probably true," admitted Mella. "Rangarirai said that the Daughters performed important ceremonies that only they knew. They were representatives of the Goddess. But, still, I want my father to be proud of me."

"If you were a Daughter of the Hunt, he couldn't help but be proud. That would be the highest of all honours."

"And Dikita would not make fun of me any more."

"Dikita listens too much to people who flatter him just to advance themselves," said Shamiso with a snort. She looked sideways at Mella to see her reaction.

Mella nodded slowly. "Yes. It's true," she said.

The N'anga did call together all the girls from Mella's age grouping before the morning meal. The girls waited nervously under the old msasa tree in the centre of the *dare*, where many gatherings took place. The N'anga conferred with Ganyambadzi and Rangarirai, while curious townspeople came, no doubt hoping to see what strange new things this unsettling N'anga had planned.

Word had got out that the Daughters of the Hunt would be restored, news that was not at all to everyone's liking. Mella could see from the look on Aunt Tongai's face that she was displeased. But many others in the town believed that they must obey the N'anga. This gathering of the girls was a necessary step for the good of the tribe and the kingdom.

Mella knew that her place was assured among the new Daughters of the Hunt, but she could not guess who else the N'anga would choose.

The N'anga stood in front of each of the girls and asked each one her name. Some answered in a clear, confident voice; others could barely mumble their names to the N'anga. One or two almost shrank back at the approach of the N'anga, but to Mella's surprise, Shamiso did not. Mella thought Shamiso would be afraid of the N'anga, but she stood steady and showed no fear. The N'anga walked back and forth, looking at each girl in turn. Who would she choose?

"Shamiso," the N'anga said. "Would you like to be one of the Daughters?"

"Yes, I would be honoured," replied Shamiso in a voice that was steady and sure.

How surprising! Mella had expected the N'anga to choose someone who was bigger and outwardly confident. But she was glad that Shamiso had been chosen. Mella felt comfortable being with her. Perhaps the N'anga could see the inner strength in Shamiso that could easily be overlooked by a less discerning person.

The N'anga did not call out another name right away. Instead she looked into the faces of the girls once again before addressing them.

"The Daughters of the Hunt will learn new skills, and they will sometimes face hardships. They must be prepared to study and to work, and often the things they learn will not be understood by those outside. The Daughters of the Hunt must be willing to face themselves, and that means that, above all else, they must have courage," said the N'anga. "Often, courage is misunderstood. Courage lies in the heart, which must possess compassion and discernment, as well as strength and determination." The N'anga stopped and stared at Revai.

Revai looked back at the N'anga.

"Revai," said the N'anga. "Do you believe you have more wisdom than the elders?"

"No, Wise One," answered Revai. "But not all the elders have the wisdom that they should."

Mella never thought that Revai would dare to utter such words outside of the girls' sleeping hut, and especially in front of the N'anga. She could see that many of the townspeople were shocked and displeased. An angry muttering started among them at the lack of respect displayed by Revai's words. The N'anga held up her hand to put a stop to it.

"You will benefit from learning lessons that are older even than your elders," said the N'anga to Revai. "You will be one of the Daughters."

Aunt Tongai caught Mella's eye. The sun sparkled off the gold bracelets glinting on the Vahozi's arms; but the look in the Vahozi's eye was not one that sparkled. Even so, now that Mella had an ally in the N'anga, someone who believed in her, Mella couldn't help returning her aunt's scowl with a smile. The Vahozi turned and stomped angrily away.

"You will eat your morning meal with me," said the N'anga. "From now on, you will eat most of your meals with me and with the Senior Sister. Your time will be spent with your teachers."

Mella, Revai and Shamiso exchanged glances. The girls usually ate their meals together, after the guests, men and elders had finished eating.

The usual breakfast was a type of thick porridge. Normally there would be milk in the porridge, but these were not normal times, and the cows had no milk to give. The N'anga and Rangarirai ate in silence, carefully placing rolled balls of the meal into their mouths and chewing slowly. Mella, Revai and Shamiso dared not speak unless spoken to. So they remained silent as well and slowed down their eating in order not to appear rude in front of the elders. Mella soon began to enjoy the slow savouring of the texture and flavour of the food in her mouth. It was as if she were learning to eat all over again, experiencing taste in a new way.

"Good!" the N'anga pronounced after everyone had finished. "You are already learning the ways of the warrior. You must pay attention to everything that you do, even the ordinary things that are done every day."

"Warriors! Are we to be warriors? Will we fight in battles?" asked Revai.

Was Revai pleased or worried at the prospect? Mella didn't know herself how she should feel about this.

"A warrior does not always fight others, although that may sometimes be necessary," answered the N'anga. "The warrior's biggest battle is the mastery of herself. That is what you will learn as Daughters of the Hunt."

"And will we also learn to play the sacred drum?" Shamiso's voice was breathless and her eyes gleamed.

"Soon," said the N'anga. "You will learn the art of the drum and the herbal arts, the secrets of the stars and the sacred songs." The N'anga paused, looking at each of the girls in turn before continuing. "These are important parts of your training, but they are useful only if you gain mastery of yourself. And to do that, you must always pay attention to everything you do. Do you understand that?"

"Yes, we understand," said Mella. The others nodded in agreement.

"I ask you: Why do you think the Daughters of the Hunt were disbanded?" the N'anga said. "What was the reason they lost their special place in the lives of the people?"

There was a moment of silence before Shamiso replied.

"Girls are not supposed to hunt. It is a man's job."

"People didn't like them," said Mella.

"People feared them!" Rangarirai spoke for the first time, struggling to her feet with the aid of her walking stick. "I remember how people feared them. I remember the relief and satisfaction of some of the people when they were disbanded. I remember it clearly, even though I was a very small girl. I could see how triumphant those people were, and I saw behind the triumph to the fear. As a little child I could see their fear, even though they wouldn't speak of it out loud."

It was hard for Mella to imagine Rangarirai as a little girl who could run and walk without her stick, whose face was smooth and whose eyes had not developed the sadness that they now held. "But why were people afraid?" Had the Daughters of the Hunt done something terrible?

Rangarirai waved her stick in front of her like a pointer. "Some people are afraid of what they cannot control. They are afraid of the ones who have mastery over themselves. The male warriors could be controlled, but not the Daughters. Some of those who feared the Daughters the most were those men who called themselves warriors."

"That is true," agreed the N'anga. "Many who call themselves warriors here have forgotten the true meaning of the word. They think that to be a warrior is only to show that they can defeat others in a fight. And they think of only one type of battle. Like those who have just now gone to the Python Healer." The N'anga's voice held a touch of scorn as she spoke these words.

Mella was aware that the N'anga was speaking of

her brother and Chiboro. She flushed at the insult, and at the same time she felt the truth of the N'anga's words. Revai caught Mella's eye. There was a trace of a smile on Revai's face and Mella knew that Revai must have been thinking that the N'anga had seen through the warriors' arrogance.

"Are you listening?" demanded the N'anga.

"Yes," they mumbled. They were ashamed of their lapse in attention.

"To be a Daughter of the Hunt, you must have complete control of your mind. You must train your body, but you must realize that it is through training the mind that the body reacts and performs the best. With a mind that is still and clear, the warrior is free." The N'anga paused again. "There is one more important thing to learn. As a warrior, you must temper your strength with love. Without love, there is no strength."

The N'anga stood, a signal to the girls that they should stand also.

"You all have so much to learn and a very short time in which to learn it," said the N'anga. "We can only make a start — one which I hope will be enough for the task ahead of you."

From that moment on, the day was filled with new activities. Ganyambadzi, Rangarirai and the N'anga introduced the new Daughters of the Hunt to the things they would now need to learn.

Rangarirai began to teach them everything she knew about the different plants. In future they would have to identify those which could cure and those which could kill and those which could do both.

Ganyambadzi took them to the forest where he began to teach them his knowledge of tracking and the ways of the wild creatures. He chose bows for them from the spares he kept in his weapons store room. These they would use in the days to come, when they would learn how to shoot. And the N'anga herself began to teach them the secret rituals of Bomu Rambi that they would carry out as the Daughters of the Hunt.

By the end of the day Mella was exhausted, but elated by all that she was learning. Even so, she could not go to sleep without seeing her father. Her father. She thought of his parched lips, his frail hands. Would he survive long enough for Dikita and Chiboro to return with the Python? She pushed down her fear. The N'anga had told her that fear was sometimes useful, but that it could also be destructive. The job of a Daughter of the Hunt was to be able to take the measure of her fear and to overcome those fears that stood in her way.

Mella slipped through the door of King Chinembira's house into the stale smell of the darkened room where the King lay. He was so still, so unlike the father she knew. A sob caught in her throat, but Mella swallowed it down and gently touched the King's arm.

"My little one, the Dreamer," he whispered, his voice so low that Mella could barely hear it. King Chinembira licked his dry, cracked lips and closed his eyes.

Mella once again took a wet rag to moisten King

Chinembira's lips. Dreamer. He had not called her that name for a very long time; not since the days when she was small enough to ride on his shoulders. In those days, the King would sometimes escape the praise singers and hangers-on and even his guard and would walk with Mella through the tall yellow grasses of the plains. Mella would chatter and the King would laugh.

"Tell me your dreams," the King would say, and Mella would relate her vivid dreams from the night before. They were dreams of adventures and wild animals and, sometimes, dreams of the ancestors. "Your dreams give me vision," the King would say. "Although I am the King and must be like a mountain to the people, I also need the time to think and restore myself, or the mountain will crumble."

"I dreamed the moon was so big, it lit up the whole mountain," Mella told him once. "But then the mountain started to move. It moved and got further away, and the moon was so small it could not light the mountain anymore. Without the moon, the mountain started to shake as if it would fall down."

The king would listen. Then he would swing Mella up onto his shoulders, and Mella would giggle as the ground receded in a whoosh, and she would find herself suddenly on top of the world. She would rest her hands on her father's head to balance herself while he held her ankles firmly. She was safe and happy.

"What do you see from up there?" he would sometimes ask.

"I see the wind running through the grass," she'd

answer.

The King had stopped walking across the plains with Mella a long time ago. Instead, he spent the time helping to train Dikita to be a warrior. Then Mella would follow King Chinembira and Dikita to the training ground, always staying several paces behind them.

In the early days of his training Dikita was proud to have her see his lessons. But later he would ignore her and pretend that she was not there. Sometimes the King would turn around and wink at Mella as if they shared a secret. Then Dikita would start to walk faster. Dikita and the King would practise with the spear or with their fighting sticks.

King Chinembira had been so busy that he had not been able to spend very much time with Mella or even Dikita. Mella saw how much her brother tried to please the King on those occasions when they were together. Dikita would become impatient when he was off his mark or could not win against his father in the fighting sticks.

Mella gently wiped the moistened cloth over the King's face. "I still have my dreams," she said. "In my dreams, the mountain does not crumble. It stays strong. One day, when you are well, I will tell my dreams to you again, and we will walk across the plains together, although I am now too big to ride on your shoulders."

Mella had often heard the praise singers telling the story of how her father had become King. This was when her brother was still a baby and she had not yet been born. Her father, who was the son of the old King's sister, had also been a member of the King's Guard.

One day, they told, the old King had decided to go hunting, and Mella's father was one of those who went with him. The hunt had gone well and the hunting party was returning to the town. They were all in a good mood, joking and laughing, pleased to be returning to their homes.

"We shall stop here," the old King announced at a ford in the nearby river. "We shall refill our water gourds and bathe before returning home."

Some of the men made a check of nearby logs to make sure they were indeed logs and not crocodiles lying in wait for unsuspecting prey. Then the party hurried to take a refreshing drink of the clear water and to cool their bodies and wash off the dust of their journey.

The old King, the praise singers told, had become stout having reached the age where a hunting trip made him very weary. He propped his spear against a large gray boulder by the water's edge; most of the others also laid down their weapons. Only Mella's father remained on guard, his fingers wrapped around the polished wood of his spear. Some of the warriors were floating on their backs in the water, where the sun glinted on the eddies and whirls of the river. The old King sat on a flat rock with the cooling water flowing over his feet and ankles.

But Mella's father could not rest. The songs of the praise singers told how Chinembira had felt sure that something was not right. He stood at the river bank, close to where the other warriors had laid down their weapons. Spear at the ready, he scanned the surrounding shrubs, rocks and tall grasses. He heard a sound like that of a bird, although he could see no birds around. Then he saw the movement of many bodies as they burst from their hiding places.

"Bandits," he shouted in warning. Chinembira immediately started throwing spears to the men in the river and ran to the side of the King in order to protect him.

The bandits were outcasts from various towns and villages who wandered the lands, preying on small groups of traders, killing and stealing. They were fierce and ruthless, but they had not counted on the fighting spirit and superb training of the men in the King's Guard. The King's Guardsmen ran forward, grabbing whatever weapon or stick was closest and closing into formation to fight off their attackers.

The bandits attempted to kill the King first. Two of them charged at the King, running full speed towards him, spears raised. Chinembira hurled himself towards the bandit who was closest to him. He felt the heavy impact jar his body, felt his breath almost knocked from his lungs, but the bandit was down, his spear knocked from his hands. The second bandit was upon the King who had almost managed to dodge aside. The spear tip that had been aimed at his heart struck higher in his chest. Chinembira saw the King fall and lunged at the bandit with his own spear. Chinembira's aim was good. The bandit crumpled to the ground, mortally wounded. By now the first bandit had recovered his weapon and Chinembira had no time to avoid the heavy metal blade. It gashed the side of his head, sending a broad ribbon of blood streaming down from the wound. Chinembira ducked, crashing into the legs of the bandit, who fell again. In the fierce struggle that followed Chinembira managed to slash the man's neck with his knife. Chinembira struggled to his feet, wiping away the blood that ran down into his eyes. All around him other bandits lay dead or were running way.

The bandits had been defeated, but the old King later died of his wounds. Although the injuries of Mella's father were severe, he was able to recover. The ancestors spoke through the elders. Chinembira was chosen as the next King for being a man of both bravery and prudence. It was his watchfulness that had prevented the party from being completely destroyed.

This story and others told by the storytellers and praise singers kept the memories of famous deeds alive to all the people of the surrounding tribes. But Mella kept her private memories to herself. She did not want to share them with anyone else.

They were memories of the walks she and the King had taken by themselves on the plains, and other memories of evenings when she and Dikita had sung together with their mother and father. The times when just the four of them had been together as a family were rare and precious. Often Mella and Dikita would sing together, their voices blending in harmony. But, like King Chinembira, Dikita no longer sang. The evenings of singing had stopped two years ago, when Mella's mother had suddenly become sick. Mella missed her mother's beautiful voice and warm soft touch, as well as the times when she had felt the closest to her brother. These were times when Dikita would lose his restless impatience and give her a rare smile.

Mella remembered the last time she had heard her father sing. Her mother had asked for a song during the last days of her illness. The King sang a song of a man who had all the riches he could want. These riches, however, could never buy what he wanted the most: the love he was to lose. The song ended. Mella saw a single tear escape from the corner of her father's eye. It ran down his cheek as he bent forward to place a kiss upon the forehead of his first wife.

Chapter 4

MELLA NOTICED, IN THE DAYS THAT FOLLOWED THE choosing of the Daughters of the Hunt, that the mystique of the N'anga settled also on the Daughters. They were treated with a new respect by almost everyone, and were greeted by their new title. They were allowed to go about their new studies without being expected to do any of their usual chores. Mella, Revai and Shamiso enjoyed their new lessons far more than household tasks, even if the lessons were sometimes difficult. Every day brought new teachings, new surprises and new wonders.

On their second day as Daughters of the Hunt, Mella, Shamiso and Revai had had their first lesson with the bow. Mella found her arms aching from the effort of pulling the string taut and keeping the bow steady. Not only her arms, but her fingers and shoulders and chest ached too.

Ganyambadzi only grunted when the girls complained of their discomfort. "Strength comes first," was all he said. All through the lesson he corrected their stance and posture and position. "Breathe properly," he ordered, "or you will never make good bow women." He sent them away to practise breathing deep in their belly, inhaling and exhaling smoothly. "And make sure it is perfect by tomorrow," he shouted after them as they left.

"Tomorrow I might be dead," said Mella, clenching and unclenching her fingers and giving them a shake. She had been gripping her bow and pulling its string for so long, she thought her fingers would stay in that position permanently.

"We shall all be dead if we're not breathing the way the Chief Councillor says by tomorrow," laughed Shamiso.

"We had better practise then." Revai stood in an exaggerated parody of Ganyambadzi and breathed noisily.

"No, no Revai," Mella interrupted. "You are not to make any noise."

They all giggled, but settled down to their breathing practice. From the corner of her eye, Mella saw the Vahozi bearing down on them like a raging hippo. Her aunt moved purposefully, heading straight towards her. Although Mella tried to concentrate on breathing smoothly, the closer her aunt came, the more difficult she found it.

Three steps in front of her, Mella's aunt stopped. Aunt Tongai had fat cheeks that puffed up when she was angry. She must have been angry now, because her cheeks were puffed out like round balls.

"If your father were well now, he would never allow you to disgrace yourself and the family in this way."

Mella watched the Vahozi's cheeks bob up and down and puff in and out, but she didn't have a chance to respond, because her aunt continued without pausing for breath.

"You are bringing shame on our heads, Mella. Instead of wasting your time doing the work of men, you should make sure you do your chores at home. Stop this foolishness now, or you shall never make a good marriage. Come with me, at once."

Mella's heart sank. Was this freedom to end so soon? Would everything be over? Her work and her effort? Was it possible that she could no longer be one of the Daughters? "Please, Aunt," began Mella.

"No." Her aunt's cheeks were enormous. "There will be no argument."

The three girls had been so intent on Mella's aunt and so distraught that Mella would no longer be one of the Daughters, that none of them had noticed the arrival of the N'anga who had appeared behind the Vahozi, as if from nowhere.

"Mella's father is unwell," said the N'anga in a voice that was both quiet and powerful, "because the people no longer honour Bomu Rambi as they should." She stepped from behind the Vahozi and stood to one side.

The Vahozi flinched and the blood drained from her face.

"If he could speak now," continued the N'anga, "I doubt that the King would condemn both himself and the land by continuing to dishonour the supreme protectress of the people."

The Vahozi recovered her composure and faced the N'anga. "It is my duty to look after Mella and prepare her for her future."

"Mella's future and the future of the kingdom are one," the N'anga answered.

"Indeed, N'anga," said the Vahozi, gaining courage. "That means that she must make a good marriage for the sake of the kingdom."

Mella felt a desperate desire to contradict the Vahozi, but she dared not. She was grateful to the N'anga, who calmly continued to dispute Aunt Tongai.

"Would it be right for the Daughter of the King not to be among those who pay the proper respect to the Goddess?"

"Does not the Daughter of the King have other duties?" countered Aunt Tongai. "Duties that cannot be fulfilled if she is looked upon as outlandish?"

"The Daughter of the King has a destiny that comes from the ancestors and from Bomu Rambi herself. These are the ways of our forgotten past. The past must be honoured or the future will be filled with sorrow."

Mella looked from the N'anga to her aunt, and back again to the N'anga. Even the King's senior wife, the Vahozi, could not argue against the wisdom of the ancestors and the word of Bomu Rambi.

"It is a great pity that Mella must be a part of this," said the Vahozi.

"Not a great pity, but a great honour," replied the N'anga. "The task of the Daughters is to re-establish the ancient ways of Bomu Rambi." Then the N'anga turned to address them all. "Is there one of you who does not feel equal to the task?" she asked.

All three girls shook their heads.

"And what of you, Mella?" asked the N'anga. "Are you afraid of being outlandish, as the Vahozi says?"

Mella didn't care what people said. She looked at Aunt Tongai, who leaned forward, her arms on her hips, her lips pursed in disapproval. Yet Mella felt only gladness that she had been saved from the Vahozi's hold. She would rather face the wrath of ten like Aunt Tongai than give up her chance to be a Daughter of the Hunt. "I wish to help my father and to serve Bomu Rambi as a Daughter," she said firmly. "That is more important to me than approval."

"Good," said the N'anga, turning away. "Come. We have work to do."

Mella's fear that her aunt would force her to leave the Daughters of the Hunt melted away and was replaced by a joy and excitement that went far beyond relief.

Mella, Shamiso and Revai filed after the N'anga, who led them through the streets of the town and out through the ornately carved archway that served as the gateway to the enclosure. They continued down the winding path that led to the bottom of the hill and into the forest. There they took a narrow pathway through the trees until they came to a clearing where ferns carpeted the ground and the sun filtered through the leaves in dappled shade and brightness. It was cooler here, a respite from the relentless sun and heat.

"There are some things that must be done in private," the N'anga told them. "These are the secrets known only to the Daughters."

"Will we play the special drum?" asked Revai.

"Not yet," the N'anga answered. "The time will come soon enough."

The secrets the N'anga first taught them were the ancient

teaching stories of the Daughters of the Hunt and the songs and chants to Bomu Rambi. They had to learn how to pitch each one just right, and they practised each part over and over again.

"Open your voice to all its strength," the N'anga instructed them. "Let it come from deep inside. Let your spirit flow through your voice."

Just as she had done when Rangarirai had taught her the song to call the N'anga, Mella felt the exhilaration of freeing her voice and sending her song to the breezes, where it drifted through the trees, across the plains and into the heavens.

@

The N'anga had made it clear to the townspeople that the primary task of the Daughters of the Hunt was to re-establish the customs of Bomu Rambi. Nothing and nobody were to interfere with their training or their duties to the goddess. Their training continued with a different focus every day.

On the fourth day after Dikita and Chiboro had gone in search of the Python Healer, the Daughters of the Hunt went again into the forest. This time it was to learn the plants with the Senior Sister and to be acquainted with the ways of the animals of the forest. It was on this day that the N'anga disappeared. No-one had seen her go. She was gone for the entire day and night. Then, as mysteriously as she had gone, she returned, with no explanation.

On the fifth day, the Daughters of the Hunt practised long hours with their bows and arrows and returned to the forest. This time it was with the N'anga, who again taught them more about the rituals of Bomu Rambi. The Goddess, who was symbolized by the moon, was also the Goddess of the animals that lived in the forest.

@

One evening as Mella hurried away from King Chinembira's house, she heard Aunt Tongai calling.

"Mella," bellowed the Vahozi.

Mella came to an abrupt stop. She suspected that the Vahozi had lain in wait for her. Although she did not dare to cross the N'anga, Aunt Tongai was still not reconciled to Mella's participation in the Daughters of the Hunt.

"Good evening, Vahozi," said Mella.

"How do you think you father would feel if he were well enough to see what you are doing?"

"He would be proud of what I am learning," Mella answered. How hard it was to keep her tone polite! Why couldn't Aunt Tongai just let her continue on her way to the sleeping hut?

Aunt Tongai glared at Mella. "When your brother comes back," she said, "and your father is well again, we shall see if they will allow you to continue in this unseemly way." The gold bracelets on her arms clinked as she gesticulated and her cheeks puffed out as a sign of her displeasure. "I will advise the King to have you married as soon as possible."

Married! As the Vahozi, her aunt would make good on her promise of marriage arrangements. She had already been making enquiries before the King had fallen ill. Mativenga, chief of one of the largest clans within the federation, was one possibility. Mella tried to keep her face from showing her dismay. She had seen Mativenga once or twice, and he'd struck her as a haughty and unkind man. He was spoken of as a person who preyed upon the weak. King Chinembira had been concerned that Mativenga might attempt to lead other clans in a breakaway from the kingdom or even try to take the leadership of the kingdom for himself. The King and his advisors reasoned that, if Mella were to marry him, it would keep Mativenga within the sphere of the King's influence, thus lessening the danger of open rebellion.

Mella thought of Mativenga's mirthless smile and greedy eyes and shuddered at the idea of being the wife of such a man. All her freedoms as a Daughter of the Hunt would be lost.

If you were to listen carefully to the rustle of the grasses as they whispered around the feet of the warriors, you would hear a single name: Mativenga …

Mativenga surveyed his rows of warriors. Nearly two thousand men were arrayed in disciplined formation in the heat of the sun-baked plain. They stood at the base of a hill, carrying on their left arms the hide-covered wooden shields that protected their bodies. In their right hands, they held the deadly iron-tipped spears that gave them renown as expert fighters.

If you could listen to the thoughts of this chief, you would know Mativenga's deepest wish — to become the new High King. Yes, it was true. King Chinembira's latest gifts of gold had not been as generous as before. Even before the King had become bedridden, rumours had swirled that the old gold deposits had been mined out, and that no new mines had been found. Mativenga had heard from a secret messenger that the King's strutting son had gone to find the Python Healer. It took a brave man to face the Python, but if it should happen that the King's son failed, why should Mativenga not be prepared to take over the kingdom?

Mativenga walked briskly as he surveyed the impressive rows of his sleek, fit warriors. His ample belly hung over the waistband that held his lower garments in place. Still, he kept himself fit, and he was a powerful man. He was well-prepared to lead his army into war. He shouted an order, his deep voice blaring through the still, hot air. The troops wheeled around in orderly formation, dust rising under their feet.

It had been necessary to decrease the food supplies of the women so that the men would not suffer during the drought. The warriors must be kept ready for the battle that Mativenga was confident he would win. After he had taken the kingdom, he would take Mella as his bride. Mativenga smiled his grim smile of satisfaction. He shouted another order. As one, the men moved at a run to the top of the hill, shields in front of their bodies, spears held aloft.

Chapter 5

In the Land of the People, the transition from evening to night could be sudden. The sun would sink in purple splendour, deepening the shadows and muting the colours. The dark would fall to be lit in turn by the glowing red and orange of the cooking fires.

It was that time of purple evening. Mella looked around at the shadows of the forest, growing ever larger and darker. Usually by now she, Shamiso, Revai and the N'anga would already have left the forest for the town.

"Tonight, we shall sleep in the forest," announced the N'anga.

Mella looked around. How easy it would be for a hungry leopard to leap on them from a nearby tree. She shuddered at the thought.

The N'anga, however, seemed unconcerned. She was already ordering the girls to make a fire and prepare their beds for the night. For their supper, they were to cook the wild birds they'd caught that day.

They searched the surrounding area for wood, collecting enough to keep their fire going for the night.

"Before we sleep," said the N'anga, "I will tell you the story of how the sacred drum came to be. Very soon, it will be time to bring the drum back to the Daughters of the Hunt."

Shamiso grinned with pleasure. Mella saw the smile and smiled in return. She knew that Shamiso, more than any of them, wanted to play the drum.

The N'anga crossed her legs and sat with her back straight. She closed her eyes. In a singsong voice she began to tell the story: "There was a time, at the founding of the empire, when the people of Bomu Rambi listened to the words of the Great Ancestor — that was when the Daughters of the Hunt were created, and with the creation of the Daughters of the Hunt, so too was created the sacred drum.

"One of the first of the Daughters was Mazviita, born to the wife of one of the greatest of the stone workers. Mazviita's father's hands were magic in patterning the walls and in creating the ancestral birds that you see, even today, on the walls of your town. These walls are older than the reckoning of even the grandparents of your oldest inhabitants.

"The stone worker was a celebrated man, but he and his wife were without children for many years. Then, to everybody's surprise, his wife started to show signs of pregnancy. And so Mazviita was born.

"She grew into a silent child, speaking little to the people around her. She would, however, speak sometimes to the spirits and listen to what they would tell her. Her father was proud of his daughter's early talent for carving. Many hours he had spent with his daughter teaching her how to carve. But Mazviita was more interested in wood than in stone. Soon she was able to carve the most intricate designs in any type of wood. The spirits of the trees guided her hands in the objects she made, which were of unsurpassed beauty.

"Mazviita was chosen as a Daughter of the Hunt. She was told in a vision that she must seek a special tree from which to make a drum sacred to Bomu Rambi. This drum was to be played only by the Daughters of the Hunt. To find the tree Mazviita had to travel far to the west, a journey that took her several months. She went by river and by land, across plains and through jungles, until she came to a grove. There she found the tree, which stood tall and straight. It was of the hardest, darkest wood, so dark it was almost black, so hard it was like iron. It was so immense that a piece of a single branch was all that was needed for the base of the drum. Mazviita asked the spirit of the tree for that piece of branch, and it was given to her.

"From the day that Mazviita left to the day that she returned, it was a full year. It was another full year before she had completed her carving of the drum. It was the most difficult and the best work that she had ever done. This very drum has been guarded by Rangarirai. It is this drum that you will learn to play."

The N'anga had finished her story, but kept her eyes closed. Mella, Shamiso and Revai wondered if she had gone to sleep sitting up. They sat in awed silence, in wonder that such a precious object would soon be delivered into their hands.

Mella looked at her companions, their faces aglow in the firelight. She felt less afraid of spending the night in the forest, knowing that they would be there.

After several minutes the N'anga opened her eyes. "We shall take turns to watch through the night, and to keep the fire alight," she said. "Keep your bow by your side as you watch, and listen to the sound of the night. You will soon learn those sounds which mean no harm and those sounds and silences that you must be wary of. Mella will go first, followed by Revai. Then Shamiso will take her turn. I will take the last watch to dawn."

The others settled down to sleep under their cloaks, on the skins that the N'anga had brought to the forest. Mella kept herself busy by keeping the fire going, occasionally adding pieces of wood to the red hot embers. She sat, legs crossed, alert and ready to spring to standing position if the need arose.

She tried to look past the ring of light cast by the fire to make out the shapes in the darkness. Was that a pair of eyes she saw gleaming through the dark? They quickly disappeared. A rustling sound had Mella leaping to her feet in alarm. It too faded away and Mella resumed her sitting position. In the distance she heard a snarl. Then it also died out. Soon Mella began to relax and enjoy her vigil. The night had a scent all of its own, subtle and sweet. Mella was sorry that she would not be able to visit her father tonight. Would he miss her presence? "Perhaps he will have seen us in his dreams," she thought. "And he will know I am here, and that I think of him."

It was true what the N'anga had said. Mella soon could pick out the harmless sounds of the night and also the sounds of alarm from nocturnal creatures. At these times, she held her bow and arrow ready, but nothing disturbed the camp. The others slept. Sometimes one of the girls would shift, but the N'anga was always very still.

How her companions had grown and changed even in so short a time. Shamiso had quickly learned to identify the plants the Senior Sister and N'anga pointed out; she could recite their uses after hearing them explained just once. Mella always had to go to Shamiso afterwards and have her explain, again, which plants healed which ailments, which plants held a poison, the effect of each type of poison and which ones had an antidote.

Revai had the gift of quickly learning how to identify animal tracks; she was by far the most skilled of the three at the bow. Mella doubted that she would ever shoot as true as Revai. Yet Ganyambadzi, in his gruff way, had assured Mella that she also was doing well.

"You will soon be as good as the warriors," he said. "And Revai will beat any one of them."

Each teacher pushed the new Daughters of the Hunt to excel, and each Daughter was rising to the challenge in her own way. But would Mella ever be better than her companions in any of the skills they were learning? It was hard to have faith in herself. Mella sighed and picked up another piece of wood to put on the fire.

When it was time, she walked quietly to where Revai lay sleeping. Mella gave her a gentle nudge. Revai shifted, but did not wake up.

"Get up," Mella whispered, giving Revai a harder push. Revai opened her eyes. At first she looked as if she would protest, but then she stood and stretched. As Revai took her place by the fire, Mella slipped under the deerskin cover. In no time, she was sound asleep.

As Mella slept, she dreamed. She dreamed that a massive snake lay in a cave. It was so still that Mella wondered if it were dead. Its skin was pale and lacklustre, scaly and dry. "It *must* be dead," thought Mella. Then the snake moved, and suddenly, it split itself open. The snake pulled itself forward, its brand new skin glowing bright and colourful as the old skin was left behind.

> *Awake the sun*
> *Bring forth the day*
> *Alight the skies*
> *O shining ray*
> *Brighten our*
> *Awake you, sun.*

Mella woke to the N'anga's voice. The N'anga sang her song of the sun in a husky contralto, and the girls knew that it was time to get up and start their day.

"Make sure that the fire is properly out," said the N'anga. "Then we will join the Senior Sister for breakfast." Mella felt her stomach growl and quickly set about scattering what was left of the embers and covering them with earth. She would be glad to have some food.

"Mella," said the N'anga. "Your gift is in the dreams that you dream."

Mella looked quizzically at the N'anga. Had the N'anga read her thoughts during the night?

"You have left your outworn ways behind you," the N'anga said. "You have put on a new way of living, as if you were putting on a new skin."

"I dreamt of a snake with a brand new skin," said Mella.

"Yes," answered the N'anga, as if she already knew. "We are helping to build new power in our old ways, even though the old ways may seem to have died."

@

It was the evening of the seventh day after Dikita and Chiboro had left in search of the Python Healer. Mella looked up past the walls into the night sky which arched over the hilltop town, enveloping everything in night's blue-black cloak.

"Nights are always clear in this drought," thought Mella, looking up at the waning moon and the bright glow of countless stars above her. "I wish for a night when the moon is hidden by cloud, and I can't see the stars. I wish that such a night would come soon."

Mella had just left her father's house with its stale, sickly smell. Her father had not moved the entire time she had sat beside him, wringing precious drops of water from a cloth onto his lips. He had not acknowledged her. "He has gone beyond my reach," thought Mella.

She was in a gloomy mood. Even though she had become a Daughter of the Hunt, her father might still die. And still there was no rain. She stood in the quiet courtyard, wrapped in the night. "My father will join his ancestors, as my mother has joined hers."

"He may be saved, yet."

Mella was startled by the voice. She turned to see Rangarirai approaching her. "Oh, I did not know I had spoken aloud," said Mella.

In her dark woven shawl, the Senior Sister appeared like a shadow against the stone wall of the partition. "I thought I would find you here, Mella," said Rangarirai. "I am sometimes sleepless, too. We have reached a dangerous point, but we cannot give up hope."

"When will Dikita and Chiboro return?" Mella asked anxiously.

"Within a few days," replied Rangarirai. "If they have not returned in that time, someone else will have to go to bring the Python Healer."

"Someone else!" echoed Mella. "But they *must* return with the Python. There is no time for anyone else to go. Who else could possibly go?"

Rangarirai did not seem inclined to answer Mella's question. Instead, she ran a gnarled finger over the smooth head of the snake that was carved on her walking stick. "The Python also is special to Bomu Rambi," she said, as if this statement served as an answer. "It is good that you are now one of the Daughters. It was your mother's great-grandmother, Mella, who gave the sacred drum into my keeping."

"Is this so, Senior Sister?" This was the first that Mella had ever heard of this.

"Your great-great-grandmother was one of the last of the

Daughters. She was my cousin. How honoured I was that one who seemed so much older and had attained so high a position would talk to a little girl such as myself."

"Why did you not tell me before?"

"I could not speak of the Daughters of the Hunt, or of the drum. It was necessary to keep it a secret. But now the time has come when it is right to tell the story that was forgotten, and to let you know of your heritage. Yes, you are a true Daughter." Rangarirai's voice was soft. There was a look of contentment on her weathered face.

"Senior Sister," whispered Mella. "You have lost your daughter, and I have lost my mother. Could we be like mother and daughter to each other?" As soon as the words were spoken, Mella wondered if it had been a foolish thing to say. *Mella of the Runaway Mouth*, she thought to herself. *Just as the Vahozi says.*

But to her relief, the Senior Sister smiled and touched Mella lightly on her hand. "Our bond is forged," she said. "Go now and sleep. You need to be rested for the work ahead."

Mella returned to the sleeping hut feeling a new quietness inside, a sense of hope and a closeness to Rangarirai. The furrow of the frown had left Mella's forehead.

@

On the eighth day after Dikita and Chiboro had gone in search of the Python Healer, Mella found herself alone in the forest. She lay face down so that she was hidden, her presence unnoticed by the chattering birds and monkeys who flitted and played in the trees. Mella felt the tree roots and the hard earth beneath her through the soft undergrowth of plants on the forest floor. Here in the forest, the effects of the drought were not so severe, although the vegetation was not as lush as it should have been. Still, it was a pleasant place to be. Mella breathed in the scents of the earth and the leaves and observed the movements of life all around her, down to the scurrying ants and beetles.

Revai and Shamiso were also out in the forest, but they were not close by, and Mella had not seen or heard either of them. She remembered what the N'anga had told the Daughters the first time she'd sent them to be alone in the forest. "You must learn to be still and to listen to all that is around you outside. But you must also learn, especially, to listen to all that is inside."

Mella wasn't sure what the N'anga meant by those words, but it *was* peaceful here, and somehow comforting. She did, however, miss the companionship of having the other Daughters by her side. In such a short time they had become very close.

Even Ganyambadzi seemed to be pleased with their progress. He was not effusive with his praise, but sometimes, he did make a grunt that could be taken for approval. "Well, well," he proclaimed. "You may yet be worthy of making your own bows. A bow made by your own hand is the one drawn the best." He had shown them how to find the best feathers for their arrows and how to make the shafts straight and true.

Yet, it was in these quiet hours alone in the forest that Mella had time to reflect on everything that was happening. This reflection was both pleasant and discomfiting. She could be proud of her new achievements — of her growing skill with the bow, her knowledge of the animals and her knowledge of the plants and herbs and their uses. But it was also in these times of silence and solitude that she wondered when Dikita and Chiboro would return with the Python Healer. How much longer would they be gone? And would they return at all?

The footstep behind her was so quiet it could have been mistaken for the rustle of a leaf in the wind. But Mella's ears had become so attuned to the sounds around her that she knew that someone or something was approaching her. Her whole body tensed, and she reached carefully and noiselessly for her bow as she turned in the direction of the sound. She couldn't see anything yet. Mella fitted an arrow into her bow and waited. She had been taught never to let an arrow fly at a target she could not see, so she continued to wait, her eyes searching the shadows beneath the overhanging branches of tress and in the bushes surrounding her.

"You listen well to the teachings." The voice was that of the N'anga. At that moment, the N'anga herself stepped into view in the space between two flowering shrubs.

Mella lowered her bow and let out a long breath of relief. "You frightened me," she said.

"But you have passed your test," answered the N'anga, "which is good. Your response was just as it should have been."

For the first time, Mella saw something that resembled a smile tug briefly at the corners of the N'anga's lips and sparkle in her eyes. But it was so fleeting, Mella could not be sure.

"I am pleased with your progress," the N'anga continued. "I have been pressing you to learn quickly. That is because your services will soon be needed. There will be greater tests to come."

Mella opened her mouth to question the N'anga, but the N'anga lifted a finger to Mella's lips and continued.

"I have a gift for you, Mella, that you will have need of."

The N'anga took from around her neck a silver crescent moon pendant that hung on a silver chain.

"The symbol of Bomu Rambi," said Mella.

"Keep it with you always," said the N'anga, offering it to Mella. "And Bomu Rambi will protect you."

Mella accepted the pendant by taking it in both hands. It is with both hands that gifts of great value are accepted, and thus Mella acknowledged the gift from the N'anga. The pendant glittered in her palm, smooth and brilliant. When she looked up again, the N'anga was gone, as though she had never been there at all.

@

The ninth day of the warriors' absence came. Tension was mounting in the town.

"Dikita and Chiboro have become lost," some said.

"No. Not lost. They have been devoured by the Python," others replied.

Stories were retold of the time when, years ago, men had gone in search of treasure reported to be in the Python's cave. But, after the men had left the town, they were never seen again.

Every night, Mella would visit her father before she joined the other girls in the sleeping hut. This night was no different. As usual, she asked the King's nieces how he fared. The answer was as it always was — the King was the same, or was becoming worse. Then Mella went into the darkened house and was left alone to sit by her father's side.

The air inside the sleeping chamber felt close and stale and oppressive. It had the scent of death to come. The King did not open his eyes, or make a move, yet Mella felt that he knew somehow that she was there.

"I wish you were as proud of me as you are of Dikita," she said to her father. His gaunt face remained expressionless. There was no flicker of recognition at her words. Mella continued to talk to him, hoping that somehow he would understand. "When you get better, you will see that I can help the kingdom as much as any warrior, for I am a warrior too. The N'anga has said that the Daughters of the Hunt are the heart of the people and hold our greatest strength. Sometimes I do not understand everything the N'anga says, but she speaks to the ancestors and to the gods, and she is surely right."

There was a movement in the doorway. Mella turned to see her cousin Fadzai, the King's niece, in the doorway, motioning for her to come. This was unusual, because the nieces always left her with the King for as long as she wanted to stay.

"They have returned," the niece whispered. "Dikita and Chiboro are here."

Surely Dikita and Chiboro would come to the King's house right away with the Python Healer! But when she left the King's side, Mella saw that people were making their way to the *dare*. Mella ran to the meeting grounds. Dikita and Chiboro stood on the raised platform with Ganyambadzi at their side. Dikita, slumped with fatigue, looked down at the ground. Chiboro swayed briefly as though about to fall. Then he straightened and looked out to the crowd. Of the Python Healer, there was no sign.

Ganyambadzi called for silence. "Dikita will now tell us the news from the Python Healer," he shouted. The crowd fell silent, and Dikita stepped forward to speak.

"Good people," Dikita started. "My friend Chiboro and I have had a very difficult journey and meeting with the Python."

The crowd was absolutely silent as they waited for Dikita's story.

"When we got to the Python's cave, the Python attacked us. We were forced to fight her," Dikita continued. "When the Python saw our bravery and strength, she declared that I must be the new King."

There were audible gasps from the crowd. A new king was never chosen before the old King was dead. The choice of the new King traditionally was always in the hands of the elders.

"These are the words of the Python," shouted Dikita above the growing murmurs. "She told us that nothing could be done for my father. That when a strong, new ruler had been chosen to lead the people, our good fortune would return. The word of the Python shall not be disputed."

Dikita turned and made his way to the edge of the platform, followed by Chiboro.

"Wait!" Ganyambadzi's authoritative command stopped the two warriors before they could go further.

"There is a question that I must ask of you, Dikita. You say that the Python has made you the next King. Listen carefully to my question. You must tell me the qualities of a good king. Are you sure that you possess them?"

Dikita stared at Ganyambadzi, his face bewildered. It was Chiboro who answered Ganyambadzi.

"It is clear that the Python has chosen Dikita because of his strength. Chief Councillor, that is the quality of a King."

"Young warriors, much more than that is needed," replied Ganyambadzi. "Perhaps when you have rested from your journey you will give me an answer."

Dikita turned to Ganyambadzi, then turned away. He took a stride towards the edge of the platform. "You tease us with riddles!" he mumbled. His tone suggested deep irritation.

"On the contrary." The authority in Ganyambadzi's voice arrested Dikita's move from the platform. "This is a time when you hold the future of the kingdom in your hands. You cannot do so without proper thought and proper action."

Dikita glared at Ganyambadzi.

"You had best not question the new King," said Chiboro in a low and threatening voice. Had his words and tone been audible to others, Chiboro's honesty would immediately have been questioned. No worthy person spoke to an elder in such a way.

Ganyambadzi showed no sign of having heard the insult. He watched Dikita's shuffle and Chiboro's swagger as they left the *dare*.

"They must rest now," called Ganyambadzi to the people. "Do not trouble them until tomorrow."

Mella's body felt numb, her mind unable to take in the news. It was hard to believe that all hope for her father was gone. But the Python had spoken. She felt a gentle touch on her elbow.

"Come with me." The N'anga was suddenly at Mella's side. She had an uncanny way of appearing when she wasn't expected. "Go to the house of the Senior Sister. I will join you there with Ganyambadzi."

In a daze Mella manoeuvred through the noisy crowd to the eerie stillness surrounding her father's house. The house was wrapped in silence like a shroud. Mella felt a tightness in her throat, but carried on to the home of the Senior Sister. Rangarirai greeted her.

"This is a sad moment," said Rangarirai. "Come in and sit down. We must wait for the N'anga and Ganyambadzi to see what is to be done next." She touched Mella's arm in a kindly way. Mella felt a small measure of comfort in Rangarirai's touch, a tiny spot of relief from the dull ache that had taken over her body.

Mella sank to the floor and crouched on the woven rug, while Rangarirai took a low stool of intricately carved wood and laid her ever-present walking stick down by her side. Rangarirai had lit a small fire which crackled and spat as it started to catch hold. These were the only sounds.

There was a movement in the door. Mella looked up to see the N'anga and Ganyambadzi. The expression on their faces startled Mella out of her daze. She read in their manner a cold anger that surprised her.

Ganyambadzi did not sit. Across the fire, he was tense, shadowy, although his voice was gentle when he spoke to Mella. "I must ask the same question of you that I asked Dikita. Tell me my child, what are the qualities of a good king?"

Mella had not spoken since she had come to the *dare*. She hardly trusted her voice and her thoughts. Finally, she answered. "A good king is one who always keeps in his heart and his mind what is best for all the people in all the tribes, and for the land and all that grows and walks on it. It is from a position of servant that he leads."

"Ah," said Ganyambadzi. Some of the tension went from his body. A look passed between him and the N'anga. "These are the very qualities of leadership that the elders consider when we choose a new king."

Why had Ganyambadzi asked her this question? Mella waited for an explanation which did not come.

"Now," said the N'anga. "It is time for us to consider the matter before us. I am not satisfied with the tale that Dikita and Chiboro have told us."

Ganyambadzi and Rangarirai nodded, their faces serious. "If the Python has spoken, surely the Python is correct," said Mella, although doubt was beginning to grow in her mind.

Mella watched in silence as the N'anga took her divining bones from the leather pouch that hung at her side. The N'anga's strong fingers closed over the bones, held them briefly and then tossed them onto the reed mat. The bones flew from her fingers and landed on the mat with a muffled thud. The fire blazed suddenly, casting long shadows on the walls. The N'anga gazed at the bones. What did the N'anga see when she looked at the bones that were scattered on the mat? One by one, she picked them up then threw them down again, studying the patterns once more. The flames from the fire dimmed.

The N'anga returned the divining bones to her pouch and looked at the faces around her. "Mella must go to the cave of the Python Healer and save her father. The King and kingdom shall die if she does not."

In the dim light of the fire, Mella looked at the three pairs of eyes which were turned on her. Surely the N'anga had spoken in jest. No-one could expect her to meet the Python alone. But the faces of the elders were serious.

"But the Python already told Dikita that she could do nothing to help. She said that Dikita was to be king," Mella stammered.

"Do you believe that Dikita speaks and behaves as one who has been chosen to rule?" asked Ganyambadzi.

Mella lowered her eyes. She didn't want to be disloyal to

her brother, although she knew the truth of Ganyambadzi's words. "Perhaps he is only tired from his journey," answered Mella. Even as she spoke, an image went through Mella's mind. She thought of Dikita on the day, just a few weeks ago, she had watched him stick-fighting with other warriors. It had been exciting to watch the skill of the young men as they clashed with their wooden staves. They feigned, parried, ducked and clashed, until a combatant was knocked to the ground or lost his staff. Mella had watched her brother fight with an intensity that sent sticks clattering from the hands of his opponents, or sent his sparring partners to the ground, one by one. She had seen the look in his eyes, a determined ruthlessness that sent shivers through her body. She shivered again. Was it possible that her brother had lied, that he would willingly let their father die?

"The spirits of the ancestors speak through the bones," said the N'anga. "They do not lie." The N'anga had not raised her voice, but there was such conviction in her tone that Mella knew there could be no more argument. It was true that Dikita did not behave as one who should rule. Mella herself would have to go to fetch the Python.

"There will be hunger and starvation soon," said Ranga-rirai.

"And war, when Mativenga rises against us," said Ganyambadzi.

Mativenga. Mella had forgotten about the rival chief, the man whom the Vahozi and her father wished her to marry. Mativenga might rise against them?

So much was happening, Mella could hardly take it all

in. "But I am afraid of the Python!" The words were out of Mella's mouth before she could stop them. They hung in the air like shadows beyond the flickering flames of the fire.

Chapter 6

If you had listened to the rustle of the grasses as they slid across the ankles of the two young warriors, you would have heard of their journey. You would have known that they started their journey with the conviction that they were the ones most able to achieve the task of bringing back the Python Healer. They were skilled in the bush, they were strong, they moved with speed; and Dikita, as the King's son, was likely to become king himself. If you had listened to the grass, you would have known that Dikita had wanted this for as far back as he could remember. You would have known that he had worked all his life to make sure that there was no warrior better than he. You would have known of his certainty that he would be chosen as the next King. But first, he had to survive the Python.

If you could have read the thoughts of the King's son, you would have seen that he was glad to have his closest friend by his side ...

THEY HAD SET OFF ACROSS THE SAVANNAH, LEAVING THE town behind them for the freedom of the open spaces. Their journey would not be an easy one, for the relentless heat of the sun had made the grass so dry and brittle that it cut their legs and feet like the blade of a knife. In some places, they saw tracts of land burnt up altogether, black and charred by fire.

They had taken careful note of the route to the Python's cave. They used the sun and the stars as their guides and the pathways of the wild beasts as their roads.

In the heat of midday, they stopped to rest under the shade of the kopje, a cluster of enormous boulders. These rocks rested one on top of the other, balanced like toys placed by a giant's hand.

"Don't drink too much water," Chiboro chided his friend. "We have to make sure we have enough to last the trip."

Dikita put down the gourd. "My throat is dry as this dirt." He picked up a handful of dry, dusty earth and let it run through his fingers. "When will it rain?"

"When we bring back the Python," said Chiboro.

"We will be heroes when we get back," said Dikita. "We will have saved the King."

"Our names will be known throughout the land," laughed Chiboro. "And one day...one day, you'll be a king more famous than your father."

"The people love and respect my father."

"But," continued Chiboro, "you will have beaten the Python. Imagine! You shall be a greater king than your father. You shall expand the boundaries of the kingdom to the largest it has ever been."

"The greatest of the kings," said Dikita, looking into the distance. But, had you heard the sounds from the kopje, they would have told you that Dikita did not see the landscape.

He saw only the images in his head, images of an immense, expanded kingdom with himself as its ruler. "Could that really be true?"

"I am sure of it," replied Chiboro, who had dreams of his own. "And I will be your Chief Councillor. Together we will be unbeatable."

Dikita smiled, pleased. "We had better get on with our journey."

The afternoon was hot and tiring, but they travelled quickly, stopping only briefly to rest and take measured drinks from their gourds. As night fell, they prepared to rest.

Dikita looked up at the vast sky that stretched over them. The stars that had guided their way glittered above. "Tomorrow, we turn northward," he said. Tomorrow would be a day as difficult as the one that had just passed, but longer, because they would start earlier. Dikita dropped to the ground and started to rub his feet. "My feet are on fire with grass cuts."

"Mine too." Chiboro started to chuckle.

"What amuses you so?" asked Dikita.

"Can you imagine the girl on this journey!"

"Mella! She would be begging to go back home by now."

Chiboro grinned. "She would not even still be with us. She would be so far behind, she would be a speck so distant that we couldn't even see her."

The warriors laughed. Soon they fell into an exhausted sleep.

The next day was much like the first, although the closer they came to the Python's cave, the more nervous they became. As night fell on their second day they were beset by cold. An eerie chill fog fell with the darkness, causing Dikita and Chiboro to shiver in their blankets, which they pulled close around them.

"I've never known it like this before," complained Dikita.

"They say that the spirits of the dead are cold," Chiboro answered, looking around him as if the spirits would materialize from the air around them.

"But we are men not afraid of the dark," said Dikita.

"True."

Huddled in their blankets, Dikita and Chiboro spent a restless night. They were on their way long before the dawn.

"Do you think it is true that the Python guards a horde of treasure?" asked Dikita as they walked, their steps slower than they had been on the previous two days.

"Maybe we will find out," said Chiboro. "It would be good to have something to show for this gruelling journey."

"Something to show greater than the Python itself," said Dikita. "We would have fame beyond all the kings."

"We would have greater fame and greater wealth," said Chiboro.

Dikita picked up his pace, his determination growing. "The greatest of all kings," he whispered, so quietly that not even Chiboro heard him.

@

On the afternoon of that third day, they came to the landmark they had been looking for: the river whose course they would follow toward the Python's cave. Dikita looked at it in dismay. The barest trickle of slow-moving water was not what he'd hoped for to refill their water gourds.

"We can climb down the bank and get some water," said Chiboro.

"It is not worth our while. We can get by on what we have. That water will be full of silt."

"You are right," answered Chiboro. "And it will take us extra time. We need to hurry to get to the Python." Even as he said the words, he suppressed a shiver.

"What do you think the Python will be like?" Chiboro asked, a little while later.

"Nothing that will be too difficult for us," replied Dikita. "We can throw our net over it and subdue it."

"I've been thinking. Maybe there is a way to approach the Python which is less dangerous."

"What do you think we should do?"

Chiboro was hesitant, but continued. "I think the Python may come willingly, if the Python is truly a healer."

"The Python kills."

"But the Python also heals. I do not think that we can so easily subdue the Python."

Dikita had always relied upon his strength in all situations. But he trusted Chiboro, whom he had known for all of his life. Chiboro often had useful ideas. "What do you suggest?" Dikita asked.

"I think we should talk to the Python and ask her to

come with us to heal the King."

Dikita gave Chiboro a look of disbelief. Chiboro continued quickly.

"We'll bring the Python an offering."

Dikita smiled. "An offering, of course. We will hunt for something when we find the Python's cave."

It was just a few minutes later that Chiboro stopped and pointed to a shape upstream by the side of the riverbank. "There's someone over there, by those rocks."

Dikita narrowed his eyes and stared ahead. "Who would be there?"

"Robbers," suggested Chiboro.

"But I only see one man."

"The others are in hiding." The ominously chill night that had left Chiboro apprehensive. It had been an omen of impending disaster.

Dikita was studying the figure in the distance carefully. "I do not think he has seen us. It is not likely anyone is in hiding."

"Take care, regardless," said Chiboro.

Dikita and Chiboro readied their spears, moving stealthily towards the lone figure on the bank. They split up so that they could approach him from opposite sides. With every careful step, they scanned the surrounding rocks, grasses and shrubs for any sign of hidden ambushers.

Then Dikita stood up and laughed, an action that so startled the bedraggled figure on the bank that his body jerked. Chiboro, too, raised himself from his crouched position, and the ragged man, wrapped in a trader's cloak, looked from one to the other without raising himself from his rest against the trunk of a withered tree. The effort of getting up seemed more than this strange man wanted to make.

"You are in cheerful moods today, my sons," said the stranger. "Always a good thing on a long journey." The man gave a severe cough, which caused Dikita and Chiboro to back up a step. Chiboro edged closer to Dikita. The man looked physically weak, but he showed no fear of them. Something about him gave the sense that he had knowledge of some inner joke that he was not about to share with the two young warriors.

"What are you doing out here?" asked Chiboro. He curled his lip in disdain, for the sinewy strength of the thin man had escaped Chiboro's notice. All he saw was the torn cloak discoloured by the dust and dirt of travelling, the worn leather of the trader's sandals, and the sick look that frightened Chiboro, as sickness sometimes frightens those who are young and have not known ill health.

"As you can see," said the stranger, "I have become ill, and had to stay here while my travelling companions, other traders, have gone on. Would you be so good as to fetch me some water from the riverbed?"

Dikita and Chiboro glanced at the embankment, which was particularly steep at that point. Dikita stepped back and motioned for Chiboro to join him, just out of earshot of the trader. "It is not wise to get too close to him," he said. "He may infect us with his illness."

Chiboro agreed. "We can't afford to be sick, and we have already wasted too much time here."

"Sorry. You must help yourself, old man," shouted Dikita, as the warriors hurried on their way. "We must continue our journey. We have an important mission."

They left the trader without a backward glance, but stopped in their tracks when his voice sounded just behind them, a quiet voice in their ears. "Remember," said the voice. "They call me the Jackal."

Dikita and Chiboro whirled around, but the trader was still sitting on the bank just where they had left him. He hadn't moved or even lifted his head in their direction. They started walking again, quickening their steps. A sense of uneasiness settled over them like an invisible haze, further dampening their spirits, as each retreated into silence.

It was some time later that Dikita stopped and looked up at the position of the sun, now sinking low. "We should have turned away from the river by now," he said.

Chiboro looked around him and groaned. "We will have to go back and find the spot. We have lost our way."

"And far too much time," said Dikita in dismay.

They turned and retraced their steps, looking for the curve in the river where they should have picked up another pathway. Neither would admit that he was unnerved and distracted by the howl of a jackal they'd heard periodically since leaving the trader. Although they looked around carefully, and held their spears at the ready, they couldn't catch more than a glimpse of a fleeting shadow, sometimes close by, sometimes far away.

@

Shadows deepened into blackness before the warriors found the point where they should have left the river to trek across the rocky ground that sloped steadily uphill.

"We had better camp here," said Dikita wearily. They knew that they would not reach the Python's cave until the following evening. It would have been less frightening to arrive in the daylight.

Again Dikita and Chiboro wrapped themselves in their blankets, but this night was no better than the one before. The otherworldly chill did not return, but it was replaced by the incessant sound of a jackal's bark. The words of the trader rang in their ears: *They call me the Jackal. They call me the Jackal.* The sound echoed through their minds. It raised goosebumps on the bodies of the young warriors and brought a chill of its own.

Chiboro tossed restlessly. His thoughts were on the Python. "I think we should go back," he said. "It's useless to continue."

"We have come too far to go back now," answered Dikita. "Tomorrow we shall reach the Python."

"Tomorrow, we may die."

"We cannot go back to the town as cowards," said Dikita.

"At least we will go back alive."

"We will not go back," said Dikita. "Unless it is with honour."

"No-one will fault us," Chiboro pleaded.

"They will say," answered Dikita in a harsh tone, "that the King's son has failed in his mission. I will not return defeated."

"Perhaps you should continue without me."

Dikita jumped up and was upon Chiboro in seconds. His strong hands closed around Chiboro's throat; his wild eyes glared into Chiboro's face. "Tomorrow, we will hunt for an offering for the Python, and you will ask her to come back with us."

Chiboro struggled to free himself from Dikita's grasp. "Dikita," he pleaded, forcing out the words with difficulty. "Let me go." Dikita let go of his hold on his neck. Chiboro rubbed his throat and neck gingerly. He and Dikita had never disagreed so violently before, although Chiboro had seen Dikita's quick temper directed at others. "Of course, you are right, my friend," said Chiboro. "I would not wish to travel back home alone. We work together, as always."

"We will be heroes," said Dikita.

"Heroes," Chiboro repeated, trying to ignore the hammering of his heart and the sound of the jackal. It was almost like a laugh that belied their words.

Morning found them already on their way, each in his own grim silence, each with his own desperate thoughts.

@

Although they stopped for only a few short minutes during the day, it was almost dusk by the time they reached the entrance to the Python's cave.

"Do you think that this is the place we have been seeking?" asked Dikita.

The mouth of the cave was narrow, only just wide enough for the two of them standing side by side, and only a little higher than the top of Dikita's head. It was a black entrance through a rocky cleft into the hillside.

"Yes, this must be the Python's lair," said Chiboro, as a shiver ran through his body. "Let us bring our offering to the Python, to keep her from harming us."

Leaving their blankets and supplies at a safe distance from the cave, they took their spears and returned to where they had seen a herd of impala. Tired as they were, Dikita and Chiboro were practised huntsmen. They crept close to the herd downwind, so that the animals would not catch their scent. Silently, they motioned to each other, choosing the young impala they would take to the Python. In one swift motion, they released their spears with deadly accuracy, sending the animal crashing to the ground and the rest of the herd into flight.

Their confidence renewed with their success, they returned to the cave entrance exhilarated and emboldened.

"We have a fine offering for the Python," said Chiboro.

"She will be pleased." Dikita kept the nervousness from his voice.

Together, they carried the carcass up the incline to the mouth of the cave.

"Let us leave it here," said Chiboro.

"A little closer." Dikita pulled the body of the impala so that it was partially inside the cave, then stepped back.

In the instant it took him to make the backward step, the Python appeared, more massive than either had imagined.

Her body was thicker than the torso of a strong man; her fierce, glittering eyes held them spellbound. Dikita and Chiboro did not stare long. The giant jaws fastened over the body of the impala and the Python was gone, back deep inside her cave in no more than the blink of an eye.

Dikita stepped forward into the cave's entrance, followed closely by Chiboro. Inside, the black darkness of the cave seemed to swallow them up. They stepped slowly, tentatively feeling their way, arms stretched out in front of them, while their feet shuffled and almost tripped over the many hard objects that littered the floor of the cave.

They stopped and waited for their eyes to adjust to the darkness, not sure if they should go further.

"Python," called Chiboro, his voice bouncing off the cave walls in an eerie echo. The echo was mocked by the sound of a jackal's laugh from just outside the cave. The young warriors could not be sure if what they had heard truly *was* the Jackal, but the sound sent their hearts racing faster and made the palms of their hands slippery with sweat. Now they could see that the cave floor glowed faintly white with bones; the bones of animals and the bones of men. At their feet lay the remains of a human skull.

Chiboro glanced at Dikita, who stood determined. How much easier it would be to turn and run, to take his chances with the mysterious jackal outside. Chiboro took a deep breath and called to the Python again.

"Python, will you help us?"

"Help us, help us," echoed in the cave. Then somewhere from the impenetrable darkness, the Python reappeared.

Dikita and Chiboro looked up to see a monstrous mouth above them and rows of needle-sharp, gleaming teeth descending towards them. The sight was so terrifying that the warriors' only thought was to save themselves from being ripped apart and swallowed.

Chapter 7

MELLA JUMPED UP FROM THE FERN-CUSHIONED GROUND. Had she really fallen asleep at a time such as this? She'd come to the forest clearing to make up her mind about whether she should go to the Python as the elders had asked. Mella looked up at the sky. The slim crescent of the moon appeared to be in almost the same position as when she had first come into the forest. She knew her sleep had been a short one, yet it had been crowded with dreams — dreams of Dikita and Chikomo fleeing from the Python.

Stars glowed white and bright while Mella stood in the centre of the clearing, her mind full of confusion. She didn't want to believe that her brother could have lied.

Find the still place. She remembered the N'anga's words. They took on a new meaning as Mella struggled to keep her thoughts from chasing around in her head like whirling tops. Taking a deep breath to calm herself, she considered what had been asked of her. Could she find her way to the Python's cave through country she had never travelled before? How could she face the Python if she did find the cave? There was so much at stake.

Mella's fingers clasped the amulet around her neck. It felt smooth and cool and reassuring. She took it off to look at it, cradling it in her palm. It glinted in the light of the brand new crescent moon above, and rays from the moon, slim and faint, gave heat and energy to the amulet. It tingled in her hand. "Bomu Rambi will protect me." The words left Mella's lips like a breath as she remembered what the N'anga had told her when she gave her the amulet.

Mella put the amulet around her neck once more and ran as fast as she could up the hill back to the town. The hill was steep to take at a run, but Mella kept going, panting as she reached the top. She paused briefly at the girls' sleeping hut. Should she wake Revai and Shamiso? Best to let them sleep. Mella headed straight to Rangarirai's house. The elders were still there, seated around the small fire. They looked as though they had not moved from their places but, in fact, they had been busy during Mella's absence.

The elders had prepared for her her bow and arrows, gourds filled with water and a bark-cloth bag that held dried beef, bread and groundnuts. They were all laid out on a cloak that would serve as a shield from the sun by day and as a blanket by night.

"You knew!" Mella said when she saw the provisions ready for her departure.

The N'anga inclined her head. "There is little time."

"Will Revai and Shamiso come with me?" asked Mella.

"No," said the N'anga. "This is a journey you must make alone."

"But why?" asked Mella. She so desperately wanted company on her journey.

"They will have their own journeys at another time,"

responded the N'anga. Mella sighed inwardly. The N'anga was as exasperating and incomprehensible as ever. How could she ask so much and offer so little?

Mella slung her quiver across her back and criss-crossed the water gourds and bark-cloth bag across her chest. She had one more question. "May I see my father before I go?" she asked as she stepped out of the door.

"You may," the N'anga answered. "But do not be long."

Mella went to the door. "*Chisara*," she called softly as she left. "Stay well."

"*Fambai zvakanaka*," the elders replied. "Go well." This was their blessing for Mella on her journey.

Then Mella was gone, walking swiftly to her father's sleeping chamber. He lay so still that Mella wondered if she were already too late in her mission. She gently touched her fingers to his upturned hand, feeling the feverish warmth of his palm. Unexpectedly, his fingers curled around hers for a brief moment before going limp once more. Mella's heart leapt at this small gesture. She must go! She must hurry to save him while there was still time. Bending to kiss his forehead, she left his house. What dreams did her father have as he lay helpless in his bed?

The night was velvet, its soft touch enveloping Mella as she rounded the curved partition of her father's compound.

"Where do you think *you're* going?" Dikita stopped Mella by thumping the heel of his palm against her chest and blocking her way. His voice was tired, and his face looked drawn.

"Dikita!" said Mella. "Why aren't you asleep?"

"There are things on my mind, Mella." For a moment Mella saw a look of regret pass over her brother's face. He dropped his hand and looked at her intently.

"Where are you going?" he asked again.

"You know what I must do now." She stepped past Dikita, who reached out to stop her. Mella pushed his hand aside in a move that set Dikita back on his heels. His expression was one of surprise. Mella turned to face him once more. "Do not disgrace the title of warrior or endanger our father's life further," she said. There was knowledge in her eyes and an assurance in her voice. Dikita made no further move to stop her. Mella continued past Dikita, leaving him standing silently. She stepped confidently on the path around the wall and disappeared quickly from Dikita's sight. She did not look back.

The night sentries watched in astonishment as Mella with her travelling provisions walked alone on the same road that Dikita and Chiboro had come by not too many hours earlier. By morning, everyone in the town knew that Mella had gone in search of the Python.

Chapter 8

Even in times of sorrow there is the seed of happiness to come. Even when there is loss, there is a gain not yet seen. Mella had gone, but the N'anga and the Daughters remained ...

"WE SHOULD HAVE GONE WITH MELLA. WE COULD HAVE helped her," cried Shamiso. "Why didn't she tell us?"

"You will help her in another way." The N'anga rested her hand reassuringly on Shamiso's shoulder. "Mella has a strong spirit, and this is her journey. We still have important work to do, but it will not take place here. We will leave and not return for eight days."

Shamiso and Revai looked at each other in surprise. Eight days was a long time, longer than either of them had been away from the comfort of their homes and the familiarity of their walled town. Spending that many nights in the bush would be a challenge. The prospect sent butterflies of excitement fluttering in their stomachs.

"Don't just stand there," the N'anga snapped. "Get your blankets and drinking gourds and food. But not too much food. I will show you how to live in the forest, even in this drought."

The girls scrambled to get their things together, along with the bows and quivers of arrows that they now always carried with them.

"There is one more thing," said the N'anga when they were ready. "We must have something that is most important to bring with us." She set off at a brisk pace to Rangarirai's house, with Shamiso and Revai following behind.

"Ah, the time has finally come," said Rangarirai with a smile. "Follow me."

Next to the house where Rangarirai lived was a smaller one. It too was round with a thatched roof, and it was decorated on the outside with patterns in earth-hued tones. But this house was a miniature version of Rangarirai's. Inside, it contained herbs and jars and cooking pots. There were also the skins which Rangarirai kept for the cooler nights of the rainy season — a season which showed no signs of coming this year.

Rangarirai motioned for the girls to step into the storage hut. It was a tight fit with all of them squeezed into the small space. There was some light which entered through a small, high window. Moving to the back of the storage hut, Rangarirai lifted a zebra skin which was covering a compartment. Shamiso and Revai could see that Rangarirai was excited, and their excitement grew along with hers. Carefully, the Senior Sister reached into the compartment, grasped a large object and hefted it into view. The drum. It was magnificent. The girls had never seen such fine carvings. It was as if the maker had brought the crescent moon from the sky and multiplied it in miniature around the drum.

In the centre of the base, curved between the moons, was a python whose body was patterned in diamonds. The mouth was open wide, showing a cavernous depth behind her sharp teeth.

"This is in your keeping now," said Rangarirai, putting the drum into Shamiso's arms. "I have longed to see the day when the drum would live again."

"It is so beautiful," said Shamiso, running her hands over the ancient wood of the darkest, hardest mahogany. "I have never seen anything to compare with it."

"I was given this in secret when I was just a young girl," said Rangarirai. "When the Daughters of the Hunt were abolished, the keeper of the drum handed it to me and told me that I was to hide and guard it. So that is what I have done, all these years. I have kept the wood oiled and polished. You can see, however, that the drumhead is old now and has fallen apart. I have lived long so that I could see this day when I can safely pass on the sacred drum."

"We will make a new drumhead," said the N'anga. "And the sound of the drum will be heard again."

The drum was heavy. Revai and Shamiso took turns in carrying it as they passed through the elaborately carved stone gateway that led them away from the town and down the winding hillside road.

"Wouldn't it be lovely to see the bright new leaves on the trees?" Shamiso said, looking up at the withered branches above their heads. The msasa trees that shaded the compound and the houses outside the walls would erupt into a blaze of orange as the young leaves came out.

"And we'd have flowers along the road as we walked," agreed Revai.

"Will they bloom when Mella returns?" asked Shamiso.

"As long as she is able to bring the Python," replied the N'anga.

The girls fell silent. Mella's journey was long; she faced many dangers. The jaws of the crocodile awaited her; the charge of the elephant and the power of the hungry lion. Mella would be alone in places she had never been before. Most worrisome of all were the terrible and inescapable coils of the Python Healer.

"Dikita and Chiboro were lucky to have escaped with their lives," the N'anga said after some time had passed. "The story they tell is utter nonsense. No-one can fight the Python and win. The Python will give help only to those who show themselves to be worthy. And that is a difficult task. A very difficult task indeed."

The N'anga's view of the Python was scarcely a cheery one.

"Do you think that Mella can accomplish such a task?" asked Shamiso.

"Mella has the capability," replied the N'anga. "As long as she remembers the lessons she has learned and keeps the pure heart of true courage."

The N'anga led them further into the forest than usual, making sure as they went along that they recognized the landmarks that would keep them from getting lost. At last, when they thought they could not carry the weight of the drum one more step, the N'anga called a halt. They had stopped at a place where the dense trees were hung with thick vines and creepers. One mossy old tree had toppled to its side, and it was here that the three rested.

"We will clear a space here," said the N'anga, "and afterwards, we will build a fire."

The girls had grown used to working hard, but today proved to be the greatest test yet of their endurance. As each task was completed, they knew with increasing confidence how much stronger they had grown.

Evening was approaching by the time the N'anga told them it was time to repair the sacred drum. Carefully, they removed the old skin from the top of the drum and buried it in the ground. Then the N'anga took out a new antelope skin, completely unblemished. They stretched it taut over the drum's opening, rolling the edges and tying them down. Then they oiled the wood of the base by rubbing it with fat. When Revai and Shamiso ran their fingers over the carved patterns in the wood, it felt as though they could hear the drum speak through the tips of their fingers.

The vibrations of the drum are its speech, but the drum must also sing. For a drum to sing it must be warmed. So Shamiso and Revai warmed the drum, turning it around and around near the heat of their fire.

"Now," said the N'anga. "We must ask the spirits if they will, once again, inhabit the drum." She placed her hands on the drum and whispered low intonations to the spirits, while Revai and Shamiso listened, entranced. Then she called them over, and placed their hands on the drum. The wood felt like flesh to their touch.

"Sing these words, as I sing them," the N'anga instructed them.

> *Open now the portals,*
> *Look upon the Daughters,*
> *Bomu Rambi Grace us.*
> *Swift spirits come,*
> *Fly shining ones.*
> *Swift ones, silent ones,*
> *Enter this the sacred drum.*
> *Light ones, shining ones,*
> *Enter now the sacred drum.*

By the time the song was over, the drum felt alive, pulsing with energy.

"The spirits have enlivened the drum and it is fit for us to play," declared the N'anga. "I will show you how to play it now. I will show you how to make the drum of Bomu Rambi sing."

The N'anga returned her hands to the drum and into her mind came the songs that were the songs of Bomu Rambi. She played the rhythms, and then had Shamiso and Revai repeat them. Hours they played, perfecting the rhythms and the techniques. They learned how, when they placed their hands in a certain way, or hit a certain spot, or bounced their fingers in a certain manner, the drum would have nuances to its voice that created its song. The notes of the drum rose into the night sky as if into the embrace of the crescent moon.

Finally, it was time to stop. As Shamiso and Revai lay down to sleep in their forest bower, the echoes of the drumbeat pulsed in their heads and drifted through their dreams.

@

There were many things for Revai and Shamiso to learn and to practise besides the art of the drum. The lessons of the hunt and the lessons of the spirit are so closely intertwined as to be often indistinguishable one from the other, which was why the Daughters of the Hunt were so named. Few knew that the real meaning of the name was to be a huntress in the quest for spirit. It was because the N'anga saw the seeds of this quest in Revai, Shamiso and Mella that she had chosen them to be Daughters of the Hunt. She saw within them the capability, the desire and the courage to do what is necessary to search beyond the surfaces of things and to find their inner secrets and inner resources. She saw that they questioned and looked for truth.

Knowing that her time with the Daughters of the Hunt would be short, the N'anga kept Revai and Shamiso in the forest. For it was here in the forest that they could receive intensive training in both the outer and inner lessons of the hunt.

Chapter 9

Even at a time when all illusions are gone, when a brother has shown himself to be a coward — even at a time like this, loyalty and love can still live …

MELLA WALKED ONWARDS, INTO THE DAWN. SHE SAW THE sky streak with bronze and orange and purple. She saw the sun break on the horizon, flaring into the sky. The stiff, dry edges of the parched grass sliced into the skin of her feet. To keep her mind from thinking of the pain of the cuts and the weariness in her legs, she listened to the sounds of the birds calling as they wheeled in the sky.

It is said that the souls of the ancestors make themselves a home in the shirichena bird whose swift, high flight makes a link to both heaven and earth. One of these Mella saw in a bright flash as it flew overhead, high in the sky.

"I wish I had your wings to fly," whispered Mella to the disappearing bird. Perhaps the ancestors heard her wish. As if with wings, Mella's feet flew with lighter, swifter tread over that hard-baked earth with its brown and blackened patches.

Mella took the pathways of the wild beasts. For many steps, her progress was watched by the sharp eyes of a lion.

From his camouflaged hiding place, he followed her, but he let her pass. Perhaps the ancestors whispered in his ear; or perhaps his heart had told him to let Mella go. It was not until the heat of midday that Mella sought a refuge from the harsh glare of the sun in the shade of the kopje. She laid out her cloak in a sheltered crevice. Had she ever felt so tired before? When she reached the Python's cave, would the Python help her? What payment would the Python exact? It was with these thoughts that Mella fell asleep.

Hours later, when Mella opened her eyes, she found the sun low in the sky. She looked about her at the strange new surroundings. Before her stretched brown, dry savannah dotted with dark gray rock outcrops, withering shrubs and the occasional gnarled tree. If only she could have had Revai and Shamiso with her. She was alone in a stark but beautiful land. This was the first time that Mella had slept alone. When she was a small child, she slept next to her mother. Then, she had joined the other girls in the sleeping hut. Lately, her sleeping mat had lain beside those of the other Daughters of the Hunt. They had become like sisters to her. But Mella didn't have time to stare long or think about her loneliness. She focused her thoughts on her father, now so emaciated he was like a skeleton. Not long ago he had been so vibrant. He had cared above all for the welfare of the people that he ruled. Her father would be strong again, as long as she did not fail to bring the Python. She would not fail him.

It had been hours since she had eaten. Mella took a long drink from her water gourd and ate some of the dried fruit and meat that Rangarirai had taken from the dwindling supplies in her storehouse. Quickly, Mella started on her way again, anxious to reach the Python's cave. As she again grew tired, she sang the chants she'd learned from the N'anga to keep her spirits from flagging. Mella sang chants to the ancestors and chants to Bomu Rambi.

> *Mothers, walk with me*
> *Fathers, walk with me*
> *Grandmothers, walk with me*
> *Grandfathers, walk with me*
> *Great Ancestors, walk with me*
> *Bomu Rambi, walk with me*
> *Walk before me*
> *Walk behind me*
> *Walk to my right*
> *Walk to my left*
> *Mothers, fathers, walk with me.*

The chants rolled off her tongue and played in the air, and her footsteps kept their steady pace. Now and then Mella passed a thorny acacia tree or went by a giant termite mound rising high off the ground. Evening was fast approaching.

It was now that Mella became aware of something which she could not see. Something was stalking her. She stopped and fitted an arrow into her bow, looking carefully around her. Slowly she pulled back the bow string. Time waited. All around her were stunted shrubs, tall termite mounds and brown and yellow grass, enough to hide a crouching predator. Mella turned to look in every direction. She remembered that no matter how quickly her heart beat or how much her fingers trembled, she must breathe deeply and evenly to remain steady.

A flash of yellow and tan streaked towards her from behind a prickly bush. There was no time to think. Mella released her arrow. A bird shrieked overhead. The cheetah swerved, and the arrow flew on to embed itself in the ground. As the cheetah turned itself again towards her, there was no time to reach for another arrow. Then the cheetah came to a stop, her eyes on Mella. For a long second, Mella looked into her dark eyes. The cheetah then turned and in one smooth motion jogged back to the bush where the spotted coat could not be distinguished from its surroundings. She passed soundlessly out of sight.

Mella let out a long breath; the hammering in her chest started to settle. Her fear was replaced by a feeling of lightness and happiness. She started again towards her destination.

@

The second night of her journey fell. Still, she did not stop.

As the night closed around her, Mella listened intently for the sounds of more predators. She peered into the darkness on all sides, looking for the glow that signalled watchful animal eyes. All was quiet. There was not even the rustle of the wind through the dry grass. Mella heard only her own footsteps crackling in the dry grass or treading on the hard earth, fissured and cracked, where there was often no grass at all.

Mella had only her thoughts for company. It became clear to her that the N'anga had known all along that Mella would have to make this journey, and that the N'anga had been preparing her for it while her brother and Chiboro had been away. Where was the N'anga? What would Shamiso and Revai be doing now? Mella thought of Revai's laugh and Shamiso's quiet strength. The thought brought her some comfort in the darkness.

Mella moved steadily forward, one hand clasped around her bow. With the other, she lightly touched her amulet. Its smooth form was a copy of the crescent that glowed above her. The moon glowed white in the dark sky, where the stars shone in their familiar patterns. Mella noted the brightest ones and the ones that glimmered more softly. There was the pattern they called the Hunter. She studied the familiar constellations, knowing that they would guide her on her way.

Mella moved past the shadowy rock outcrops and the stark, dark forms of trees silhouetted against the night. A rustle in the darkness made her stop and once more raise her bow. The sound died and Mella lowered her bow again. She feared the predators of the night, but most of all, she feared the Python, feared the price that she would have to pay for seeking the Python's help. Mella was also afraid that she would lose her way and not reach the Python's cave in time to save her father. Was she on the right track? Over and over she recalled the instructions of the N'anga. She hoped she was going the right way, but she could not be certain.

The next day, after her midday rest, Mella came upon the riverbed whose course she knew she must follow for a while. It was then that she saw him: a slight ragged figure not far ahead of her. He sat with his back to a tree, his cloak pulled around him. He did not get up as Mella approached him.

"Good day, my daughter," he said to Mella as she came closer. His voice was weak.

"Good day, father," she replied. "What brings you here alone?"

"I might ask the same of you," said the trader. "But I see that you are in a hurry, so I will be brief. It is a sickness that has caused me to be left here while my companions travel on. I will rejoin them soon." At this, the trader wheezed a sickly cough.

This man looked so weak. Why had his companions left him alone in this condition? "Is there something I can do for you?" Mella asked.

The trader held out his empty water gourd. "Be so kind as to fetch me some water from the riverbed."

"Here, take this," said Mella, pouring water from one of her own gourds into his.

"And what of you?" asked the trader.

"I can fetch more from the riverbed," said Mella.

The trader looked towards the sluggish water that was all that remained of the once mighty torrent that had coursed between the banks. "Yours will surely be murky with sand."

"No matter," said Mella. "I can strain it and perhaps dig underground for some more. I hope that soon I will reach my destination. Is there something further that I can do for you? Have you need of any food, father?"

"Nothing more," said the trader. Mella blinked. The man's voice seemed much stronger already. And the hand that reached for his walking stick no longer shook. "I have food enough. Blessings on your journey."

The trader smiled his mysterious smile, as though enjoying a joke. "Watch for the jackal, my child," he said. "The jackal will be your guide." He waved her onwards.

Mella continued along her path beside the river, with the trader calling blessings to her as she went, his voice surprisingly powerful. What a strange man. He looked emaciated, yet perhaps there was more to him than she could yet determine. What did he mean about the jackal? Mella gave a shrug; by now she was used to riddles. A few seconds later, she rounded a curve and saw a large, lone jackal trotting ahead of her. He kept his distance, but never strayed. Occasionally, he would stop and look back in her direction before trotting on again.

At another bend in the river, the jackal veered off on a different path and sat down a few yards up the path as though he were waiting for her. "This must be where I leave the river," thought Mella. She refilled her empty gourds, then set out confidently behind the jackal. The jackal was truly her guide, just as the trader had said. Who was that trader? Where had he come from? So many riddles to puzzle through.

As night fell, Mella started to slow down. Her feet, which had moved so swiftly, felt like boulders, her legs wooden.

The jackal stopped at an enclosed circle of protective stones, just large enough to lie in. She had been travelling for four days. They seemed to be endless. Could she continue at this pace? Mella sank into a comfortable space between the boulders and ate hungrily. She didn't care that the bread was stale. The food made her feel sleepy and in no time she was in a deep sleep.

"Mella." Mella heard the N'anga's voice speaking to her through the fog of sleep. "Mella." The N'anga had spoken again. The N'anga was there. Mella saw her; saw the smooth black skin of the N'anga's face, the plume of the black ostrich feather and the movement of the N'anga's sinuous limbs. The N'anga was dancing in the night. She moved with ease, her arms, head and body curving and undulating exactly like the movements of a snake. She danced, and then she stretched out her hand to Mella. "Come," the N'anga invited. So Mella joined the N'anga, following her movements until her own became as smooth and snakelike as those of the N'anga. On and on they danced the snake dance. It lasted through the night.

When Mella opened her eyes with the rising sun, all tiredness was gone. Had she really spent the night dancing with the N'anga? She looked around, her eyes scanning the ground around her and the slopes of the hillsides and plains. The ground was undisturbed and bore no marks of dancing feet. On the hills beyond there was no sign of anything that resembled the figure of the N'anga. Only the jackal, lying there, flicking his ears by a rock. Mella shook her head.

"Good morning, Jackal," she said brightly.

The jackal flicked his ears some more, but did not get up.

Mella stood and stretched her arms towards the big red ball of the sun, and moved them with the flowing, sinuous movements of a snake. The actions of the night came back in a rush. She was doing the snake dance, but why? Mella stopped in wonder, but she didn't have time to wonder for long. The jackal had got up and was trotting off into the distance. Mella quickly gathered her bow and quiver, her drinking gourds and bark-cloth bag, and followed the jackal, jogging quickly in the bright dawn.

Their journey was steadily uphill. *We should arrive at the Python's cave today*, thought Mella. And then? Mella's throat went dry. She took a long drink from her water gourd. She must hurry now. The jackal was moving on ahead of her. He led Mella through boulders and rocks, up the narrow path already taken by Dikita and Chiboro.

Mella could see it as she approached. The dread was like a vapour surrounding the shadowy cleft embedded in the side of the hill. The mouth of the Python's cave lay before her, just as the N'anga had described it. Its narrow entrance was not inviting. Mella felt her heart beat faster as she approached the opening. Nervously, she peered into the blackness of the cave and took one tentative step forward. For one brief moment, she thought she would turn back. Then she remembered her father's face when last she saw him. No. She could not give up on him no matter the sacrifice she had to make. But surely she did not have to take this on by herself. The jackal: perhaps he would help her. She stopped to look for him, but the jackal was gone.

Chapter 10

When the dry, hot wind rises, it sweeps across the valleys and hills, the towns and savannah. It carries with it the harsh sounds of betrayal ...

"THE FOOLISH TWITTER OF OLD WOMEN PERSUADES YOU more than the word of a warrior." Chiboro faced Ganyambadzi, his eyes ablaze with anger.

"You dishonour the name of warrior," replied Ganyambadzi, "when you are disrespectful of the elders and speak in such a manner to the chief of your people. I stand in the place of the chief, and respect is my due."

"It is time you proclaimed a new chief, instead of hanging onto power yourself," interjected Dikita. The two young warriors stood side by side, their bodies tense, their hands restless at their sides. Ganyambadzi stood solemnly, spear in hand.

The three were behind one of the lower interior walls that provided privacy around the dwelling of Ganyambadzi. In the quiet that followed the finish of the midday meal, no-one else stirred.

"Why are you in such a hurry?" asked Ganyambadzi calmly.

His calm infuriated the young warriors all the more.

"Have you not heard?" shouted Dikita. "Mativenga is preparing for war. More tribes might follow his lead, and the federation will be broken."

"I have heard," replied Ganyambadzi, "and have sent emissaries to negotiate."

"Talk! What good is that? We need a show of force." Dikita's sneer showed disdain for the weakness of Ganyambadzi.

"If Dikita were King," said Chiboro, "he would put down all rebellion. No-one would dare to break away."

Ganyambadzi shook his head. "Do you remember when I asked you what were the qualities of a good king?"

"That! What of it?" Dikita's voice was increasingly impatient.

"You did not return to me with an answer," said Ganyambadzi, still calm. He leaned on his spear and continued. "If you believe that force alone can rule a nation, you will achieve nothing but bloodshed, and you shall prove yourself unfit to rule."

"It is you and the dying King who cannot rule," said Chiboro.

"The King is not yet dead," said Ganyambadzi. "He is still the King, and I am still his Chief Councillor."

Chiboro snorted with disgust. "And while you wait, the kingdom withers and dies."

"All will revive when Mella returns with the Python," Ganyambadzi answered.

"Mella will never bring back the Python," Dikita said.

"You imagine that a girl could do better than we?"

Chiboro was clearly outraged.

"Perhaps," said Ganyambadzi, his voice quiet and confident, his look penetrating. "Perhaps she has more courage than you."

"You dare to question our courage?" Dikita exchanged a look with Chiboro. Ganyambadzi had guessed their secret. In a rage, Dikita lunged at Ganyambadzi with his spear.

A slower man would have been pierced through, but Ganyambadzi was fit and agile. He dodged out of the way and thrust his own spear at Dikita. Ganyambadzi's spear grazed Dikita's arm. Dikita had quickly swung to the side and aimed again for the Chief Councillor. But Chiboro had already jumped at Ganyambadzi and, wrapping his arms around the Chief Councillor's legs, had pulled him to the ground. Dikita swung at Ganyambadzi's head with the shaft of his spear, knocking him unconscious.

"Quickly," said Chiboro. "He must be gagged and tied. Then we must take him away. It would not be good for blood to be spilled here, or for anyone to know what we have done."

They carried him away, wrapped in a blanket, beyond the walls of the town to a small hunters' hut.

In the afternoon lull, no-one saw them. It was half an hour before Ganyambadzi regained consciousness.

"We will not release you until you declare Dikita King," hissed Chiboro to the Chief Councillor as they left him firmly tied in the remote hut.

"What if he refuses to declare my kingship?" Dikita asked as they walked back to the town.

Chiboro's answer was terse. "We will have to kill him."

@

Dikita was silent and thoughtful on his return to the town. He sent word that he would address the people on an important matter. As the townspeople gathered in the *dare*, it was a subdued and worried Dikita who addressed them.

"I have come to tell you," announced Dikita, "that Ganyambadzi has appointed me head of our people while he is away. As we know, my father is very sick and I have been named the new King by the Python. Ganyambadzi is most worried about the fate of Mella. The foolish girl has gone to the Python's cave and Ganyambadzi has decided to go in search of her and bring her back, rather than have her throw her life away needlessly. He feels that he will be able to catch up to her as she is, after all, only a girl. We can only hope that they do not both lose their lives."

Rangarirai looked around at other elders in the crowd. It was clear that they were puzzled that Ganyambadzi would leave without first consulting them. But with Dikita in charge, there was little that the elders could do even should they, like Rangarirai, not believe Dikita's story. They would have to wait until the N'anga's return. But the N'anga had not been seen at all in the days of Mella's absence. She and the two remaining Daughters of the Hunt spent all their time in the forest, far from the town. They would not return for many days.

@

That evening Dikita and Chiboro paced outside the hut where they had tied up Ganyambadzi.

"Our plans have all gone wrong," said Dikita. He snapped a small twig in half. His hands were restless.

"Mella should not have gone for the Python," said Chiboro. "We did not expect that our story would not be believed."

"Why would Mella make such a pointless journey? She must know that she cannot bring the Python," said Dikita.

"There is no doubt she will be killed by the Python." Chiboro turned to face his friend. "And we must kill Ganyambadzi."

Dikita flinched. "So many deaths. There is nothing that we can do for my father, but let us not yet kill Ganyambadzi. My position will be better if it is conferred on me by Ganyambadzi. The other elders are under the sway of the Senior Sister, and we know that she opposes us. Ganyambadzi must declare me King."

"I do not believe that Ganyambadzi will keep quiet about what has happened," said Chiboro. "We must arrange for him to disappear for good. But we will wait until the N'anga has gone far away."

"The N'anga will not stay long after she returns with those girls," said Dikita. "After the N'anga goes away, we will put a stop to any plans to bring back the Daughters of the Hunt. But for now we will pretend that we accept what the N'anga has said. It's a good thing that there will only be two girls to deal with."

"Mella won't come back," said Chiboro. "And if she does,

it will be without the Python. She will have no power."

Dikita nodded. "There is no turning back for us now."

Chiboro caught the reluctance in Dikita's voice. "Don't worry. I know the loss of your sister is great. But soon you will be King and all will be right."

@

There are always those who do not question what they are told. Many in the town did not doubt what Dikita and Chiboro had told them. They were sorry that Mella had left to risk her life on an impossible mission. They hoped that she would see the senselessness of her quest and return before she was harmed. These townsfolk kept an eye out for Mella as the days passed, hoping that Ganyambadzi would find her and bring her back before she was consumed by the Python.

There are also those who know to look beneath the surface to see the truth. The elders and some of the warriors both young and old saw that the words of Chiboro and Dikita did not ring true. They questioned quietly among themselves and waited to see if Mella would return in time to save the ailing king.

Then there are always those who will make up stories and spread false rumours. Some in the town said that Mella had perished, either on the journey, or upon reaching the Python. They said that she would not return.

There were many worries for the people of Mopo-poto — the scarcity of food and water, the lack of pasture for their cattle and their lack of gold and trade goods. It had been many weeks since anyone had seen any sign of the traders who came from the north and the east, bringing an array of silks, rich cloths, cookware and colourful glazed pots to exchange for iron, gold, ivory and skins. But the animals that provided the ivory and skins had all gone, and the mines were exhausted of their gold and precious metals. No new mineral deposits could be found, no matter how hard the people searched. The women who usually worked in the mines found other tasks to fill their days.

In the days while the N'anga and the Daughters of the hunt were gone, Dikita further rationed food to the townspeople. He allocated smaller proportions to all except for the warriors, who were kept in intensive training so that they would be ready for battle. He put out the word that no tribe would be allowed to break from the union, and recalled the emissaries who had been sent to Mativenga by Ganyambadzi. Only those who were able to observe Dikita carefully would have seen his disquiet. He spoke bravely, issuing orders that all the warriors must prepare for war with Mativenga. He began to make arrangements for an elaborate funeral for the time when his father would die.

Mativenga continued with his plans for the overthrow of the kingship. The alliance that was the kingdom of Chinembira would soon disintegrate. The kingdom moved nearer to war, and every day the King slipped nearer to death.

Chapter 11

The keen-eyed birds of the sky observe matters far below them. If you are one to whom they will speak, you will learn of many things ...

MELLA FOUND THAT HER LEGS WOULD NOT MOVE. AT THE cave of the Python, all thought except the awful power of the Python was blotted out. She would surely be entrapped within those massive coils, squeezed lifeless and devoured. If the Python had declared Dikita King, then Mella would pay for her doubt of him by being killed. Maybe her father was already dead. But Mella had felt the King's fingers close around hers; she had felt his blessing even as he lay between the world of the living and the dead. She knew that she could not turn back from her mission. Her father lay emaciated and still in the heart of her homeland.

Mella struggled to remember the lessons of Ganyambadzi and the N'anga. She knew that she must reach the still place within where all was clear and calm, and she remembered the amulet from the N'anga, her symbol of Bomu Rambi.

Mella's fingers closed around the crescent moon, a silent prayer for protection forming in her mind. The Daughters of the Hunt had faced danger before. The N'anga believed in her, or she would never have sent Mella on this journey. Revai and Shamiso believed in her, as did Ganyambadzi and Rangarirai. She felt their belief flow into her blood, giving her courage. Mella took a deep breath and stepped forward into the impenetrable blackness of the cave.

"Great Python," she called, her voice barely above a whisper.

All was silence. Mella's heartbeat sounded loud in her ears in the still of the black cave. Soon that sound was drowned out by the sound of the bones crunching under her feet. She advanced further, taking tentative steps, and as her eyes adjusted she started to make out the pale forms of the human and animal bones that lay on the floor of the cave. She stopped momentarily. Was that a sound? The air smelled dank. She would suffocate in this close tomb. She swallowed. Even that sounded loudly in her ears. Slowly, she continued, threading her way through the bones that lay all around and in front of her.

"Great Python," she called again, louder this time, stopping to listen for any sounds.

Without warning, the Python appeared before Mella, entirely filling the space in front of her. Mella could see nothing except the scaly pattern of the Python's massive body. The Python's giant head was only a hair's breadth away from Mella's face, her flickering tongue darting so close that Mella felt the breath of its motion across her cheek. She was held motionless in the glare of the Python's eyes. These were eyes that glowed fierce and wild, untameable and primal. Mella wanted to run, but could not move. She tried to speak. No sound came from her mouth. From deep inside her, Mella summoned the will to try again.

"I have come to ask for your help." Mella heard her own voice as if it were far away. "Will you return with me to cure my father and save the land?"

"Mella." The voice of the Python was like the whisper of wind and fire. "Do you not fear that I will crush the breath of life from your body? Are you not afraid your bones will join the others remaining here in my cave?"

"My love for my father is stronger than my fear." Mella clutched her amulet tightly. She spoke without wavering. She knew that a false word or a false step would be her death.

"What have you there?" asked the Python.

"It is the symbol of Bomu Rambi."

"Child, do you not know that it is dangerous to wear her symbol without the proper knowledge?" hissed the Python.

"It is true Great Python. I am ignorant still, but I am one who wishes to learn," Mella answered. "The Great N'anga has taught me, and gave me this symbol because I honour the Goddess."

The Python and Mella stood motionless one in front of the other. Mella dared not move. Without warning, the Python turned and moved deeper into her cave. "Follow me," she instructed.

This was the time to turn and run, but Mella knew that she could never outrun the Python. She knew, too, that to run now would mean the end of her father's life, so she followed. The Python moved far more quickly than expected for one her size. Her heart pounding, Mella followed her deeper into the Python's cave until it widened to an oval. There the cave gleamed and glowed from a mysterious light. Piled high around the walls were mounds of diamonds, sapphires and other precious stones, as well as stacks of gold and silver jewellery. Mella had never seen so many riches. She let out a gasp.

"King's Daughter, all that you see here can be yours," said the Python.

Large clusters of gold towered above Mella's head. When she looked up at the glinting gold, her breath caught in her throat.

"You can be rich, King's Daughter. You can have more riches than anyone you know," continued the Python, "if you wait here until your father dies. You can take this treasure and be Queen of your people. All you need to do is to wait for his death, and that day will be soon."

The Python wanted her to let her father die. It was not possible. The Python was supposed to be a healer.

"But," stammered Mella. "I came to save my father."

"To save your father?" The Python seemed almost to laugh.

The N'anga had said that the Python would save the Kingdom. The N'anga could not be wrong.

"Yes. And to save the land. It is dying with him, and so will the people. I need you to help me."

The Python moved so that she blocked the view of the glittering treasure. "What makes you think that I will help you?"

Mella could not give up. She had believed so strongly that the Python Healer would help her.

"The N'anga has told me that you can heal my father," Mella said, with more confidence than she felt.

"You will give up the treasure?"

"Yes, gladly, if you would help my father," Mella answered, her voice growing desperate.

"Are you sure that is what you want?"

"Yes, Python. I am sure."

Had her answers satisfied the Python? Would the Python now help her? Mella could not be certain. The Python was starting to undulate her body in slow, rhythmic, wavelike motions. The movements reminded Mella of the dance that she had been taught by the N'anga. This was surely the same dance that she had learned in her sleep. Mella instinctively followed the Python's movements in the dance. As soon as she started to move, Mella felt a lightness in her body. She knew now that the N'anga had taught her the dance for this moment.

Suddenly, Mella felt as if she were surrounded by light. She danced in a space of sound and silence. She became part of the light and the dark, the waters and the tides, the winds and the earth, all that grows — fire, air and all of creation. All of this danced and swirled around her and through her and became, at last, the massive form of the Python.

The Python stopped moving as abruptly as she had begun. Mella almost fell to the ground, her head spinning.

She heard the Python's voice, as though the Python spoke directly into her mind. "Turn around."

Mella did as she was told and felt the Python's silky skin and heavy coils wrap around her body. She waited for the coils to tighten, but they did not. The Python's voice hissed in her ear.

"I will heal your father. And when I have healed him, you and I shall return to the cave. Do you agree?"

Mella nodded.

"Then you must carry me."

Carry the Python? It wasn't possible! The Python was at least three times her weight. Nonetheless, she would have to try. Bound in the coils of the Python, Mella took her first, laborious steps. She turned toward the mouth of the cave in the direction of home.

Chapter 12

The birds and the winds are not the only ones who speak.
Others carry messages in secret …

MATIVENGA BRUSHED A FLY AWAY FROM HIS FACE AND motioned for the newly arrived messenger to sit.

"So, the King's son has returned without the Python," he said, repeating the words of the messenger. "You have earned a reward."

Mativenga fingered a nugget of gold that lay among others in an earthenware bowl. "Any other news?"

"The King is expected to die very soon," said the messenger. "And even though Dikita says that the Python has made him the next King, Ganyambadzi has not named him to succeed Chinembira."

Mativenga held out the gold nugget.

"Many thanks, Chief Mativenga," said the messenger.

"You may go." Mativenga waved his hand dismissively. He had recruited the spy from Mopopoto months ago, but now had no further use for him. Mativenga stood and went to the door of his house. He would mobilize his army immediately.

@

Within the uneasy heart lies the hope that in action, there might be a way to legitimize that which is wrong. Dikita held such a heart, though he hid it well.

He paced in front of his massed warriors, standing thousands strong with their skin-covered shields and iron-bladed spears. "The Kingdom is betrayed by Mativenga," shouted Dikita. "He marches towards us even now." Dikita, with Chiboro at his side, wore his leopard-skin tunic, as did the other members of the King's Guard, who were lined up in front of them. Other warriors, not within the Guard, wore tunics of water buffalo hide, or were bare-chested. The evening moon was growing round, approaching fullness. It shone down on the assembly of men who waited eagerly for Dikita to lead them in their assault against Mativenga and the rebel warriors.

Women, old people and children had also gathered to see the departure of the army.

"We will show them who rules," shouted Dikita.

"It is not you who rules. The King still lives. It is the King who rules." Rangarirai had stepped forward, in front of Dikita. She looked small and frail next to the tall, solid, fierce warrior. Yet she showed no fear when she faced him. She turned towards the army of warriors and raised her walking stick into the air. The polished wood gleamed in the pale moonlight and the carved snake that curled around it gave every appearance of coming to life.

"We are safer in our fight if we wait behind these walls. Dikita has no authority to take this action," said Rangarirai, her voice strong and clear. "Ganyambadzi is the only person, save the King, who can permit such a step. Neither the King nor Ganyambadzi would do so without consultation with the elders and myself. Do not forget that without the blessings of the ancestors, you are sure to be defeated."

The army of warriors shifted uncomfortably. It was true; the elders and the Senior Sister should have been consulted. Dikita looked as if he would strike Rangarirai. This was a direct challenge to his shaky authority.

The power of the ancestors is great. Their protection extended to the Senior Sister whose title was also the Great Ancestor. Even Dikita could not be seen to dishonour the Great Ancestor. Yet he was dangerously close to an act that would bring dishonour down upon himself.

Chiboro moved forward and spoke up, clearly anxious to prevent a rash act by Dikita.

"Dikita will soon be King," declared Chiboro. "The ancestors have already given him their blessings through the Python. It is his right to take any action necessary to save the kingdom. He must act now."

"It is not his right." Rangarirai's voice was softer than Chiboro's, yet her words carried force. "Only Ganyambadzi has that right. It is he who stands in the place of the King."

"Ganyambadzi will never come back," shouted Dikita.

"How is it that you can be so sure?" Rangarirai's question had the tone of an accusation. It was not missed by anyone who heard it.

Dikita clenched his fist and moved toward the Senior Sister. His heart was pounding so loudly he could hear the pump of blood rushing in his ears. There was a collective gasp from the townspeople. Dikita stopped.

Rangarirai held up her stick. "Listen," she said, her voice still clear and unperturbed.

The sound of the blood rushing in Dikita's ears had been replaced by the steady beat of a drum. Everybody heard it now: a powerful rhythm, deep and booming, from a single drum.

"It is the sacred drum of Bomu Rambi," announced Rangarirai. "It lives again after all these years."

@

The vibrations of the earth itself will tell you of the footsteps that walk upon it ...

The first steps from the cave and down the hilly ground felt unendurable. How could Mella ever complete the journey in enough time to save the life of her father? But she did not complain. Step by step, she struggled to carry the Python's great weight; many times she staggered. Surely she would drop before long.

Yet, within an hour, the ache in her arms and the strain on her body had lightened. The Python was becoming easier and easier to carry. To Mella's great surprise, the longer she carried the Python, the lighter the snake became. How could this be? The size of the Python had not changed. The snake was as massive as ever. She was coiled many times around Mella, leaving only her legs and head free. Even her arms were encased in the Python's coils, yet Mella was able to walk easily.

By the evening, Mella was moving ahead with all the speed of her outward journey. Her feet felt quick and light. She hardly noticed the weight of the Python at all, although she was always aware of the Python's presence.

The Python did not speak to Mella on the journey. A menace radiated from the very being of the Python. And although Mella felt that menace at all times, it was this same menace that kept her safe from predators. Mella was certain that, even without words, the Python was guiding her on her journey back.

Mella had only her thoughts to occupy her mind through the days that followed. Each day, as she saw the sunset, or the new sunrise, she drew nearer to her home. Would her father still be alive? Would she be in time to save him? Mella's thoughts and dreams became as jumbled as her days and nights. She hardly knew or cared which was which. All she knew was that she must keep on until she reached her home.

Was it during the day or was it at night that she dreamed of Ganyambadzi, wrapped in the coils of a rope just as Mella herself was wrapped in the coils of the Python?

There came a day when the sound of a drum beating in time to the rhythm of her heart brought Mella back to the knowledge that she was awake, walking in the light of the day. She heard the drumbeat before she saw the three figures who waited for her. Its sound helped to drive her forward.

"I am getting close to home," Mella thought. The end of her journey was coming closer. "Who is playing the drum?"

It could not be anyone who was in the town. The drumbeat sounded too close for that.

Then she saw them up ahead. There was no mistaking the tall, straight figure of the N'anga with her plumed headdress. Beside her stood the stocky form of Revai and the smaller, compact Shamiso, who kept up the steady rhythm on the drum. The fog in Mella's mind began to lift at the sight of them. The first smile in days came to her face as she reached the waiting figures.

Without a word, the Daughters of the Hunt stepped into place on either side of Mella. At another time, perhaps Revai and Shamiso would have run from the vision before them. They both caught their breath at the sight of the huge snake wrapped around their friend. They dared not look into the Python's cold and unfathomable eyes, which glared from her massive head, while her tongue flicked the air. The N'anga took her place behind Mella, and in this formation they made their way towards the hilltop town shrouded in the fast-falling evening.

As soon as she saw the empty houses that lined the hillside road, Mella knew that something was wrong. No children played outside. No adults sat and talked in friendly groups. The houses were much too quiet. Something must have happened. Her father must have died. There could be no other explanation for the quiet. She looked up at the imposing walls at the top of the hill, but they gave her no clue as to what was happening behind them. After all she had gone through, she was too late after all. Too late, after such struggle!

Mella turned her head to look at Revai and Shamiso. She could tell that they were also worried. They had quickened their pace. Mella struggled hard to keep up with them. With the Python coiled around her, she could not turn around to talk to the N'anga without falling behind, and she did not want to do that. Did the N'anga know what was happening? The N'anga said nothing.

There was a blast of a horn from the guard tower. "Mella has returned," shouted a voice from the tower. "She has brought the Python."

The news was echoed within the walls and quickly spread throughout the town. By the time Mella and her companions had reached the *dare*, she could hear the buzz of astonished voices. People drew back as Mella approached, keeping well out of the Python's reach. Children cried and hid behind their mothers, but none were more astonished than Dikita and Chiboro.

Mella came into the open space of the meeting ground to see the warriors massed and ready for battle. The diminutive figure of Rangarirai stood defiantly in front of them. Rangarirai was almost dwarfed by Dikita, yet she stood her ground as Mella approached with the Python. Dikita had stumbled backwards in an effort to get further from Mella and that which she carried. Chiboro's mouth hung open, his eyes round with disbelief.

"Welcome, Mella," said Rangarirai, her eyes sparkling in her wizened face. "You are just in time."

Even before the Senior Sister had finished speaking, Mella felt the pressure release from her body as the Python dropped to the ground. In the quickest of motions, the Python hurled itself onto Dikita. He toppled onto the hard, dry earth, unable to scramble away. In less time than a blink of an eye, Dikita was encased in the coils of the Python. Mella could only watch in horror as the Python closed her mouth over Dikita's head.

"Please, I beg of you, let Dikita go," Mella cried. She ran towards the Python. Would she be able to stop the Python? She could not bear to watch her brother die, especially in such a horrifying way.

Then the Python did something unexpected. She removed her mouth from Dikita's head and relaxed her hold to the point where Dikita was able to breathe. The blood had drained from Dikita's face, which was a mask of terror. He was still held firmly within the Python's massive coils. The Python's mouth remained wide open over his head, and the warriors had all fallen back, shouting and scrambling to get as far away as possible.

"Will you spare Dikita?" asked Mella. Only she dared to come close to the Python. "I do not want to bring death to my brother."

"He will have brought death to himself." The Python's voice was like a breath, but still clearly audible.

"I will bring back Ganyambadzi if you release me," Dikita gasped, his voice no more than a hoarse whisper.

The Python let go of Dikita, who struggled weakly to his feet. "Tell the people what you have done," breathed the Python again.

Dikita took a step back from the Python and looked

around at the expectant and puzzled faces on every side of him. He lowered his eyes and started to speak. "Chiboro and I were frightened by the Python," he mumbled.

"Louder," shouted a voice from the crowd. "We can't hear you."

Dikita shuffled uncomfortably, glanced at the Python and quickly looked away. He raised his voice to speak again. "We ran from the Python. We were afraid that she was about to kill us. She did not tell me I would be King. I made it up because I did not want to show how we had failed." Dikita bowed his head and kept his eyes lowered.

"There is more to tell, I believe," said Rangarirai. "What of Ganyambadzi?"

"Chiboro and I have made Ganyambadzi a prisoner because he would not declare me King. He is safe. We will return him to the town. I will go right away," said Dikita taking another step away from the Python.

"No." The Python whipped her tail around Dikita's legs, causing him to fall again. "Chiboro will go and you will stay."

Chiboro had been edging his way to the back of the crowd hoping to escape from the Python unnoticed, but he stopped stock-still when he heard the Python's words. He was immediately grabbed by two other warriors who held him firmly between them.

"Of course I will go," Chiboro's voice trembled. "I will bring Ganyambadzi back at once."

"There will be nowhere to hide if you fail to do so," breathed the Python again.

The warriors who held Chiboro let him go. He turned towards the gate and broke into a run.

Mella didn't wait until he was out of sight before turning to Rangarirai. "What has happened to my father?" she asked. "Is he alive?"

"He is alive," said Rangarirai. "But barely so."

The Python had already released Dikita for a second time and was moving rapidly towards the house of the King. Without stopping to look at her brother, Mella ran after the Python, who was soon out of sight.

"King's Daughter, you must wait." The N'anga was calling her. Mella stopped and waited for the N'anga to reach her. "We will go to the King's house, but we must keep our vigil outside."

"May I not see my father now?"

"The work of the Python is not for any mortal eyes," replied the N'anga. "Only the Great Ancestor and the Daughters of the Hunt may remain here with me. Revai and Shamiso will play the drum as a call to Bomu Rambi."

When the N'anga and the Daughters of the Hunt arrived, the King's nieces and guards left the King's compound without argument.

Revai and Shamiso took turns with the drum, keeping their rhythm going through the night outside the door of the King's house.

Mella sat down with her back against the wall, listening for any sounds inside. It was so still that she wondered whether the Python was doing anything at all. Successful or not, what would the Python demand for the task that she performed? The long days and nights of travelling had taken their toll. Even as she struggled to stay awake, Mella's eyes closed. She slept to the steady beat of the drum.

@

A story is told by those who had only vague memories of tales once told that the Python requires a sacrifice for every act of healing, and that the sacrifice must be pure. Mella had been asked by the Python Healer to return to her cave and had agreed. Everyone knew of the bargain that had been made. It was expected by these same people that Mella would pay with her own life for the miracle of saving her father.

In the darkness of the night, a breeze began to blow throughout the land. At first, it was so slight as to be barely noticeable, but it grew stronger. The deep darkness of the night sky faded into dawn, and with the dawn came a bank of cloud.

Mella's eyes flew open. How long and deeply she had slept! Someone had covered her with a zebra skin. There was a scent of moisture in the air. Rangarirai and the N'anga sat nearby. The drum still kept its steady beat, but something had made Mella wake up — a sound from her father's house. It was hardly more than a shuffle, but Mella was instantly awake and alert. She sensed, more than saw, a movement in the doorway of the King's house. Mella scrambled to her feet, pushing her zebra skin cover to the side.

The drumbeat stopped. This man, so thin and gaunt —

surely he was no more than the ghost of her father? Mella stood motionless. No; she would not cry out.

Her father's skin was ashen. He was able to stand only by leaning on the side of the doorway. He looked as if he would fall if he let go. His hollow cheeks were caved in, making his cheekbones stand out. The King turned his eyes on his daughter. From the sunken sockets, there was a renewed spark. In that spark was the father she had known before. No, this was no ghost. This was truly her father.

Something splashed on Mella's forehead. Then there was another drop, cool, sudden and surprising. Then rapidly more and more splashes on her head, shoulders, back and arms. She held up her face to the sky and spread out her arms. Rain had finally come to the parched land. Rain at last! Turning briefly from her father, Mella saw old people come out of their houses to dance in the rain. Grown men and women ran into the courtyards and open spaces, cavorting like children. Young children shrieked and jumped, holding up their faces to the water that cascaded down on them, washing over their bodies.

Mella laughed, her hands held upwards as though to pull the water from the sky. She turned towards her father. He had moved outside to stand without the support of the doorway. His body seemed to drink in new life with the water. He was truly cured! Mella ran towards him now, then stopped short. How weak he looked, as though he would fall at the slightest touch. King Chinembira opened his arms to welcome Mella. She stepped forward and placed her own arms around his thin body. The arms that held her were bony, and the voice that spoke to her was hoarse and unaccustomed to speech, yet it was unmistakably the King's voice.

"Mella," he whispered, "continue to walk the dream paths."

Chapter 13

There are those who do not read the signs of the sky and the clouds. They do hear the stories that come in whispers with the rain ...

MATIVENGA'S ARMY, READY TO BEGIN THE ASSAULT ON THE capital of the kingdom, was halted by the rain that poured over them. It soaked their garments and made their shields heavy with the weight of the water infusing the dry wood and skin.

Mativenga raised his face to the sky. This rain had come suddenly. It was a sign of something, although whether it was a good or a bad sign, only time would tell.

"Continue to advance," he ordered his men, whose orderly formation had broken up in disarray. "You must maintain your lines."

Drenched and bedraggled, they came to the foot of the hill and heard the horn blare from the town walls. It would be impossible to storm the walls in this downpour. His army was at a great disadvantage.

Mativenga's vast army stretched out behind him. Through the cascading rain a small group of people were visible waiting just outside the town gate, looking down on his assembled men. Along the walls were warriors armed with bows and spears. There were only two choices. Mativenga could attempt to storm the town, or he could take a select group of warriors to meet with the delegation at the gate. He took only a moment to decide: better to find out what the delegation had to say.

Taking his most trusted warriors with him, he began the climb. As he approached the town's entrance, he could make out the composition of the group that awaited him. This was not what Mativenga had expected. Ganyambadzi was there, to be sure, but with only one other warrior. This was not the King's son. Also, there were three girls, each armed with a bow. One was the King's daughter. She and one of the other girls had fitted arrows into their bows.

The smallest girl carried a drum which she had begun to beat. The drum sounded through the rain and its beat carried over the men assembled at the bottom of the hill. *Defeat, defeat*, it said to them, over and over. The men began to look around at each other and then to fidget. With every stroke of the girl's hand on the head of the drum their position became weaker. *Defeat, defeat*: the sound came faster.

These were the words which the drum spoke to Mativenga, and the words of the drum were true. He continued to climb the hill and, on reaching the gateway, laid his spear in front of the King's Councillor, bowing as he did so.

Mella had watched the approach of Mativenga. She saw now that he would not bring his army to attack her town.

"We come to enquire after the King," said Mativenga. "And to pledge our allegiance to him."

"We hope that your allegiance is as strong as the rain that falls," replied Ganyambadzi. "The King's strength returns."

There was no longer any chance that Mativenga could take over the kingdom. Although Mativenga smiled broadly, Mella noticed that his smile did not touch his eyes. She heard the falsehood in his oily voice.

"I would hope to cement our allegiance by a marriage to the King's daughter," said Mativenga. "Please pass on my request to the King, along with my greatest respect and wholehearted gladness for the return of his health."

Mella's face remained impassive, although every part of her being wanted to scream *no* to Mativenga's words. He was repulsive, false and duplicitous. She stared coldly at him. He had only glanced briefly at her; he directed his attention and remarks solely to Ganyambadzi.

"I will relay your message to the King," said Ganyambadzi.

Mativenga waited. A tribal leader and his retinue should always be invited to stay the night as a guest of the town, but Ganyambadzi did not offer the customary hospitality. This slight, with the collapse of Mativenga's plans, would mean a grave loss of stature in the eyes of his people. Word would reach the towns and villages throughout the kingdom. Mativenga bowed to Ganyambadzi, turned and walked back down the hill. His chosen band of warriors followed silently behind. The girl's drum still beat out its ominous message with every step that they took.

As Mativenga and his retinue reached the bottom of the hill, the drumbeat stopped. He faced his warriors, who waited in formation. On Mativenga's approach, they had come to attention, their thoughts unreadable in the set of their faces. Mativenga turned around to look back up to the gateway. The delegation was nowhere to be seen.

@

Mella waited under the cover of a palm-topped shelter just outside the King's house. The elders had gathered inside, and of course, Ganyambadzi and the Senior Sister were there too, with the N'anga and the King. Mella had taken her crescent-moon pendant from around her neck and clutched it tightly in her hand.

"Please let them say I don't have to marry Mativenga." Mella offered her prayer to the ancestors and to Bomu Rambi. "I could not stand it."

Surely the N'anga and Rangarirai would speak on her behalf, but would their voices prevail against those who would send her to Mativenga? She knew the Vahozi would urge that the marriage contract be made. Was this to be her fate? Were her days of freedom as a Daughter of the Hunt over? Mella could hear voices inside, but she couldn't make out what was being said.

From under her shelter, Mella watched the rain, lighter now although some of it still splashed, muddy, on her legs. A cessation of the voices inside caught her attention, and she looked through the rain towards the house. The elders were leaving. She counted them as they left in single file. They walked past Mella, but said nothing. Then Rangarirai stood in the doorway. What had they decided? Would Rangarirai be the one to break the bad news? Mella looked at her face, but could tell nothing from the Senior Sister's expression. Rangarirai motioned for Mella to come forward. Mella felt her legs trembling. She didn't want to know her fate, not if it was to be with Mativenga.

Breathing deeply and forcing herself to stay calm, Mella stepped into her father's house. She could see that he already looked stronger, although he remained seated. Once more he was dressed in a fine silk robe woven through with golden thread. It hung loose on his body, but the hand that held the royal staff was firm.

"Come forward," he said to Mella.

She stood in front of him, watching carefully, preparing herself for the words that she feared the most — the news that she would soon be the wife of Mativenga.

"I thank you for all that you have done," said the King. "I know that your loyalty to the kingdom is strong, and that you have risked your life to save it."

It was so quiet in the room, Mella could hear herself breathing. There was only the King's voice, raspy from so much time in disuse.

"We know that a marriage to Mativenga would ensure that he remained harmless," continued the King. "But the benefits to your remaining a Daughter of the Hunt are much greater."

The King smiled at his daughter. "You shall not marry anyone against your will."

Rangarirai smiled too. Mella beamed back, her face alight.

@

On the morning of King Chinembira's healing, amongst all the celebration, a question could be heard in the town of Mopopoto: *What would be the fate of Mella?* She had escaped marriage to a man she loathed, but what price would the Python exact?

@

At first, the ground, baked hard as an earthenware pot, resisted the assault of so much rain beating down on it. Water ran in sheets across it, until finally, softened, the earth allowed itself to take in the moisture and drank deeply, allowing plants to unfold, releasing their fragrances into the air. Riverbeds started to fill so that the animals, too, were able to drink, and regain strength and vigour.

@

Clouds still covered the sky on the day Mella was once again to undertake the journey to the Python's cave. But there was a break in the rain after a day of downpour. Water ran in rivulets through the streets of the hilltop town and washed the accumulated dust from the stone walls. Even the stone ancestral birds, perched on the top, seemed to be refreshed. The land would soon come alive with colour. The sweet scents of flowers and fruits would fill the air. Mella looked around her. Would this be the last time she would see her town, her home? At least her last view would be of a town returning to life. She must go with the Python, whatever fate her going would bring. After all, it was because of the Python that the rains had returned and her father was healed.

The Python wrapped her heavy coils around Mella once more and Mella took the first laboured steps on the trip back to the Python's cave. Once the journey started, however, the Python again became lighter. Mella was soon walking with ease. The Python was no more communicative on this trip than she had been on the journey to the town. Why had the Python wished her to go back? What would happen when they reached the cave? The Python's silence did nothing to lessen Mella's fears. Mella had heard the stories that the Python usually required a sacrifice. Although she felt that the Python did not want to harm her, she could not be sure. Who could be sure of the Python?

If Mella had not been troubled by the unknown intentions of the Python, this could have been an enjoyable journey. The land had come to life in a burst of green and orange and red. The grass returned, the msasa trees took on their new spring leaves, and the scarlet-coloured lilies bloomed almost overnight. Fissures that had torn apart the ground had now closed as if they were wounds that had healed, leaving no scars.

It was a bright new world that Mella travelled, so much so that she still had to rely on the Python's silent guidance to find her way back to the cave. They passed the kopjes and the riverbed that now ran with clear, fast-flowing water until, at last, they started the uphill climb towards the mouth of the cave.

@

Mella stood, once more, at the entrance to the Python's cave. The morning was bright but, at the opening to the cave, darkness seemed to swallow everything inside. In the morning light the Python's skin shimmered as the sun glinted off the yellow and brown diamond pattern. The Python stretched herself out. Mella, now relieved of the burden of carrying the Python, grew even more tense. What would the Python do now?

"Great Python," she ventured, her voice small and tentative. "I will bring you an offering for curing my father."

"That is not necessary," breathed the Python. "Follow me."

The Python disappeared into the darkness of her cave, the whole length of her enormous body vanishing in one flash of movement.

Mella wondered if she were going to her death. Would she be the sacrifice? What else could the Python mean when she said that no offering was necessary? Mella stepped into the darkness of the cave, her eyes straining as she tried to avoid the bones that lay on the floor. She was lost in the darkness, following the faint echo of the Python's command. "Follow," she had said.

Follow for what reason? Mella tried to steady her

breathing and keep calm. Then, as unexpectedly as before, the cave widened and Mella found herself in the glow of the inner cavern. After the darkness of the outer tunnel, the brightness of this cave was almost dazzling.

The Python lay in front of the mountains of glittering jewels, regarding Mella with her terrifying eyes. She raised her head so that she towered over Mella.

"King's Daughter, you may choose any of these treasures for yourself," the Python said.

Mella looked around her. There were gold nuggets, flashing diamonds, deep green emeralds, bright silver chains and bracelets and so much more that Mella couldn't take it all in. The light glanced off a large pile of diamonds. They were as big as her fist. Mella slowly made her way over to it and reached out her hand to touch one of the stones. It felt cold and hard. The jewels were beautiful, but Mella preferred the beauty of the forest, surrounded by its scents and colours and the chirping of birds. These were the treasures she longed for the most. She had no need for gems or gold. She looked at the Python.

"Python, I do not want any of these things," she said. "The greatest gift was the life of my father and to see the rain and the return of life to the land."

"But there is one thing you must take," said the Python. She held in her mouth a silver chain. On it dangled a gleaming crescent moon, exactly like the one she had been given by the N'anga. This was a gift that spoke of the protection of both Goddess and Python. This was a gift that she would always keep close.

Mella held out both hands and allowed the Python to drop the amulet into her palms.

@

The smell of shame and regret is strong. It hangs like a fog that will not disperse ...

Dikita and Chiboro closed the gate to the cattle pen. Evening was gathering and the cattle had been herded back from the day's grazing.

"Chiboro," Dikita motioned for his friend to come closer and looked around to make sure that nobody was near. "I will not stay to do the work of boys." The two warriors had now been stripped of their honoured place among the Guard. Dikita felt the eyes of the townspeople filled with scorn when they looked at him. The people of Mopopoto humiliated Dikita by turning their backs when he came near them. He was no longer a warrior. Worse, he had lost the respect of his father.

"We have stayed too long, already," agreed Chiboro. "Perhaps we can join the traders and become rich."

Dikita shrugged. A trader was not a warrior. Many times he had been forbidden from an audience with his father; many times he had choked on the bitterness of the knowledge that he would never be King.

The muscles in Dikita's face tightened. A familiar look of anger came to the face of the King's disowned son.

"Let us leave quickly," urged Chiboro.

Dikita threw down his staff and left it lying in the grass. The two former warriors left the cattle in the pen and took the direction that would lead them to the coast. They would never be able to return; they would say no goodbyes.

Chapter 14

Sacrifice. The word rang often through the streets. In the town of Mopopoto, it was said that King Chinembira had lost both son and daughter ...

THE MOON CYCLED, FADING INTO BLACKNESS THEN WAXING full again. It was on this night of the bright full moon that Mella approached her home again, eager to see her father and her friends. She had been walking quickly, but stopped when the walls of the town came into view. She gazed at the dark towering shape silhouetted against the bright night sky. She could even make out the shapes of the giant stone birds keeping their guard over the town's inhabitants.

"The ancestors watch over us," thought Mella. There was a breeze in the night air that brushed her skin with pleasant coolness and brought the scents of leaves, grasses and night blooms.

"Mella!" Shamiso and Revai were running towards her on the road.

"The N'anga said to look for you on the full moon," puffed Revai when they reached her.

"We knew you would come." Revai embraced Mella. Revai joined them and the three of them held each other in an excited jumble.

"Where is the N'anga?" asked Mella when they let go of each other.

"She has gone," said Shamiso.

"Gone?" Mella exclaimed. She felt a pang in her chest. She owed so much to the N'anga. Had she ever thanked her?

"She said we did not need her any more," said Shamiso. "But Rangarirai has been teaching us many things, and she taught us the song."

"The one I used to call the N'anga?" said Mella. The grief inside her lessened.

"Only if it is truly necessary," said Shamiso.

The three girls started back along the road, talking as they walked.

"You were gone so long," said Revai. "What were you doing all that time?"

"I was learning much from the Python," said Mella.

Shamiso and Revai looked at Mella in amazement.

"I have so much to tell you," said Mella. "But first, there is something I must give you from the Python."

Mella took two chains from around her neck. Each one held a shining silver crescent moon.

"The Daughters of the Hunt will wear these to show that we are special to Bomu Rambi," said Mella. "The Python will protect us."

Revai and Shamiso took their chains and slipped them over their heads. From that day onwards, they always wore the symbol of the crescent moon.

EPILOGUE

I am the N'anga. I can tell of many tales. I can tell of the young women of the Land of the People who returned to the newly remembered ways of Bomu Rambi. I can tell of a morning of celebration ...

HUGE CROWDS GATHERED IN THE *DARE*. VISITORS HAD BEEN arriving for days. Added to the usual population were the rulers and dignitaries of chieftainships from all corners of the kingdom.

People jostled and swayed to the sound of drums and listened to the praise singers who were singing songs about Mella's adventures with the Python and about the prosperity the Daughters of the Hunt had brought to the land.

In the years that had followed her journey to the Python, Mella had made sure that the Daughters of the Hunt were restored to their full role in the life of the kingdom. It was the job of Revai and Shamiso to choose three new girls every year to join the Daughters of the Hunt and to teach them the ways of Bomu Rambi. They looked for girls with courage and spirit, who possessed keen intelligence. These were girls who were not afraid to question, and who held a strong determination to uphold the integrity of the Daughters. Sometimes, girls were chosen from among the other tribes in the kingdom. There were always many contenders for one of the coveted places. The Daughters of the Hunt continued the rites of Bomu Rambi and the kingdom had grown to become stronger than ever.

Although this morning was one of celebration, for Mella, it also held some sadness. It had not been long since the death of her father, who had lived well these past years and had died a peaceful, natural death. After a meeting of the elders, Mella had been declared Queen in recognition of her courage and good judgement.

Mella was about to start on the procession to the *dare*. She stood on the highest point of the hill where she would now live in the large house of the ruler. The house, although grand, was also a little lonely. Like the mountain top the house represented, the ruler had to be a mountain to the people. Mella breathed in the morning air and looked around at her loyal Guard in their leopard-skin tunics. Sometimes she wondered what had become of her brother, who had once worn the leopard skin so proudly.

A palanquin waited for her. She stepped into it, smoothing her robe of delicate white silk woven with colourful turquoise and crimson patterns.

Around her the dancers moved to the rhythm of the drums and to the words of the singers. In front marched the Daughters of the Hunt.

The procession reached the raised platform in the *dare* where the old tree spread its sweeping branches, its leaves rustling in the light breeze.

Mella had a fleeting thought of the dream she had had the night before. Occasionally, Mella would still dream of the N'anga. In this dream, the N'anga had said that there would be a time, long after Mella's reign, when the beautiful land once again fell on times of disaster. It would be a time of disease, of rulers who abused their power and built up riches for themselves while the people suffered. It would be a time when the word *justice* had no meaning except to bolster the power of the leaders. In that time there would be another call to gather the Daughters of the Hunt. For again, the ways of Bomu Rambi and the path of the Huntress would be lost, and the sacred drum and the crescent moon would have to be carefully guarded, in secret.

Always, there would have to be a someone who could hand on the secrets to brave young women who could hear the call or the ancestors and the spirits, who were not afraid to take up the challenge of becoming a Daughter of the Hunt. But that time of loss and sorrow would be far, far in the future.

Mella lightly touched the silver crescent moon around her neck and stepped up onto the podium.

I am the N'anga, magician and storyteller. I have told you that Revai and Shamiso would have journeys of their own, and this is true. Each has a special place in the memories and on the tongues of the Daughters of the Hunt. But theirs are other stories which, one day, I may tell. For you see that I am, among other things, a weaver of words, a maker of magic ...

END

Other Books for Young Adults from Sumach Press ...

- SERAPHINA'S CIRCLE
Fiction by Jocelyn Shipley

- WHEN GROWNUPS PLAY AT WAR
A Child's Memoir by Ilona Flutsztejn-Gruda

- TIME AND AGAIN
Fiction by Deb Loughead

- THREAD OF DECEIT
Historical Fiction by Susan Cliffe

- CROSS MY HEART
Short Fiction by Jocelyn Shipley

- THE PRINCESS PAWN
Fantasy Fiction by Maggie L. Wood

- OUT OF THE FIRE
Fiction by Deborah Froese

- GETTING A LIFE
Fiction by Jocelyn Shipley

- THE SECRET WISH OF NANNERL MOZART
Historical Fiction by Barbara K. Nickel

- MIRACLE AT WILLOWCREEK
Environmental Fiction by Annette LeBox

- THE SHACKLANDS
Historical Fiction by Judi Coburn

- SWEET SECRETS: STORIES OF MENSTRUATION
Edited by Kathleen O'Grady and Paula Wansbrough

- ALL THE WAY: SEX FOR THE FIRST TIME
by Kim Martyn

Find out more at www.sumachpress.com